TWENTY-SIX

PLUS

ONE

BY

DESTINY ROSE

This book is a work of fiction.
Names, characters, places and incidences are purely down to the imagination of the Author.
Any resemblances to actual events, places or people, living or dead, are coincidental.

No part of this publication may be reproduced, stored in a database (computerized/digital or otherwise) and/or published by print, photocopy/computer internet/eBook, audio media, microfilm, or any other means, without prior written consent of the author.

Copyright ©2003Elizabeth Bernadette Barry
Cover artwork with permission: M.P. Elliott: Northern Artist

Thank you to Siobhan for guidance
Special thanks to Rachel for encouragement
xx
Special thank you to Dan Clyburn. Author of the book
'Far Away Planet' for friendship
Rest in peace Dan
xxx

For you, me, her and him
xxxx

CONTENTS

Chapter 1-----------Lost
Chapter 2-----------Deminick City
Chapter 3-----------The Truth
Chapter 4-----------The Plan
Chapter 5-----------Connections
Chapter 6-----------The Journey
Chapter 7---------- Little Hampton
Chapter 8-----------Answers
Chapter 9-----------Face to Face
Chapter 10 ---------Miracles can happen
Chapter 11----------Hope
Chapter 12----------Visions
Chapter 13----------Memories
Chapter 14----------Acceptance
Chapter 15----------The calm
Chapter 16----------Knowledge
Chapter 17----------Surringer
Chapter 18----------The Unexplained
Chapter 19----------The Secret
Chapter 20----------The End

Note from Author
Poem by Author
About the Author

Destiny Rose

CHAPTER ONE --- LOST

"WHAT THE HELL?" Laura shouted, she had crashed into a low wooden fence in front of a group of trees, smoke was rising from the bonnet, her hands were still holding the steering wheel, and she couldn't remember anything. Dazed and shaken she stumbled outside. Skid marks went up the embankment to the motorway which was now about fifteen feet away, she rushed up to the road and was thankful that no-one else was around, the last thing she wanted was to be found, she was trying to disappear without a trace and until now she had been careful.

Her home and husband in Deminick City, over 400 miles behind her, but still not far enough. Looking down she made sure hip bag was tied securely round her waist, it was 5.40pm by her wristwatch, she took a suitcase out of the boot and the last thing she did was to throw her car keys into the group of trees.

Quickly she made her way along the grass verge, trees lined a fence for as far as she could see. Looking behind her, she checked making sure no-one had discovered the car then threw her suitcase over the fence and climbed it. Inside the woods, her grip on the suitcase was firm, and its little hard steel wheels held out well as she rushed on the dishevelled uneven ground. The sky's light was disappearing the more the trees enveloped her, and darkness started to surround her, then memories of the last few days back home returned and the night her husband tried to strangle every breath from her body. They had gone out for a meal with his business associates and wives, something the men arranged every now and again. The ladies chatted amongst themselves and the men talked business. It was 10pm when they got home, and Laura had no idea what he had in store for her. Inside the apartment she hung up her coat and calmly he said.

"Laura, come over here for a moment please." Smiling, thinking he was going to hug her after a pleasant evening she walked over to him, but, as soon as she was in front of him, he slapped her hard across her face. The force from the blow sent her flying backwards and she fell onto the floor. Immediately and with force he pulled her up and onto her feet, blood poured from her nose, but neither the sight of it or the fact that she was half unconscious stopped him from slapping her again, only this time he held her up, so she couldn't fall back down.

Fiercely, he shoved her up against the wall, then he put his hands around her throat and started to strangle her. She couldn't breathe, and his grip was tightening. Her mind was in utter turmoil; she tried desperately to force his hands away from her throat, but he was far too strong. She couldn't kick out because he used his body to keep her pinned against the wall. She felt sure she was going to die and with eyes pleading she begged him to let her go, but he was like a man possessed. Staring wildly at her, his eyes were black and full of hate, his words rang loudly in her head.

"You bitch, you dirty, filthy bitch, you couldn't keep your eyes off him, you should have looked away, you whore." She didn't know what he was talking about. He continued to tighten his grip on her neck until her body went limp, then he let go of her and she fell to the floor.

Her friend Kay had promised to ring her to see how the meal had gone, but she kept getting her voicemail, she felt worried so made her way to the apartment. The door was left on its latch and she found Laura in a terrible state. Laure told her he had left her unconscious on the floor. Kay told her she would stay with her that night even if he came back, but he didn't come back and they both knew she had to leave him. Bret was getting more violent towards her, and one day she may not be so lucky and wake up from one of his attacks, so with Kay's help they planned her escape. They decided to leave her credit cards, her passport and driving license; anything that could lead to her whereabouts. Laura had enough cash to get her over for a few weeks and decided to sleep in the car if necessary until she could find some work.

Laura had spent the entirety of her childhood in the care system, surrounded by other children, she didn't like to get to close to anybody and mostly kept to herself. She left the home at 16 and was 17 when she met Bret, and they were married within a few months, she was now 26. Bret David was her first serious boyfriend and the only person she had ever gotten close to. When they first met, he made her feel happier than she'd ever felt before and when they married, she thought he'd be her partner for life. But slowly, she learnt that wasn't to be. Their relationship wasn't good or true, it was bad and an unhappy lie.

In the beginning, he quickly became overprotective; wanting to know where she was going and who she was with, but then he started despising her, he didn't like her talking to people for too long. It could be staff, customers at their nightclub or even friends. Behind closed doors he would grab hold of her wrists hard and push her, or curse in her face. If she had been too long at the shops or at an appointment, or even took too long making a drink in their kitchen, he would blow up in a rage. Little reasons that should hold no significance whatsoever, but to him they were like the end of the world. Over the years she tried to find solutions to help him overcome his negative behaviour, but it didn't work, she grew weary of fighting against who he had become. Laura's spirit had broken years ago, but her mind was still strong enough to say, enough was enough. Then her thoughts were suddenly broken, as she saw an opening coming into view through the trees.

'Thank Goodness, she was sure there would be a farmhouse or an inn, but as she walked onto the field her heart sank at the sight because ahead and all around for miles was nothing but grass, acres and acres of uninhabited greenery. Dropping her suitcase on the floor, sluggishly she sat on it and put her head in her hands. It was now 6.50pm and she was utterly exhausted. She had been running on nervous energy for days and not eating or sleeping properly. Tears filled her eyes, but she refused to cry; crying wouldn't help her. Losing the car was a big setback and one she hadn't anticipated, and now she was lost. She didn't want to go back into the trees and didn't like the idea of walking the empty fields. What on earth was she going to do? She looked up to the sky, at least it wasn't raining, so she should be thankful for that, and then as if some deity had read her mind it started to rain. What the hell was coming next for her?

Feeling defeated she took a lightweight hooded rain coat out of her case and put it on. Then took a bottle of juice and a snack from her bag and sat their eating and drinking in the rain. After a few minutes something startled her as it raced out of the trees to her left. It was a white cat, it stopped in front of her, stared wildly and then raced into the group of trees to her right! Maybe that cat was going home to get out of the rain? Quickly she gathered her stuff and rushed in the same direction as the cat. The trees gave shelter from the downpour which she was thankful for, but there was no sign of the cat.

(One good thing in her country Kaffanderim, was the fact no large, wild animals ran free. The biggest thing would be a fox, and they were not going to stop her journey. Her country was

Destiny Rose

twice the size of Great Britain and shared similar weather, but unlike the latter, anything grown and produced here stayed within it. They were the only self-sufficient country in the world.)

Before long the ground gradually became softer; it felt like walking on a woollen carpet instead of the hardened soil she'd gotten used to. Then the floor turned into hard stone and with her next step she lost her footing and slipped. She screamed as she fell backwards, her head hit the hard floor with force then her thoughts were no more…

7pm, and Ray Maitland was driving home after another long day in the office the weekend was upon him and he felt relieved. Marcy, his housekeeper would have gone home by now he usually caught up with her in the evening; however, after stopping at the crash scene earlier he was running late. The police had stopped everybody traveling along the route in hope of gaining information about the car found abandoned.

Ray knew the police of Little Hampton well, and although he couldn't help them. he was sure they would solve their puzzle soon; he had left his job as a police sergeant in the city he was born and raised over 8 years ago, 14 years he had given to then job and now was 39 years old. Never married, no children and was an only child, his parents were both retired and living abroad.

Ray's father had taken him fishing in Little Hampton many times, when he was a child a charming and peaceful village which Ray had always loved and one he would settle down in, and found the perfect house on the edge of the woods, and he found suitable premises for his new business in of the neighbouring village of Great Oak. When his security business was up and running, he put an advert for a housekeeper in the post office

Destiny Rose

and Marcy applied. His thoughts turned to Marcy and he was hoping she would have lit the fire for him before she left this evening, a warm fire and a glass of cool red wine was all he wished for right now.

Marcy was walking on her garden path as the rain began. Luckily Ray's house was just a short walk through the woods separating their gardens, she was sixty-six years of age and loved her job as housekeeper, cleaning came easy to her and she enjoyed it. Over the 7years she had become like a mother figure to him, which was endearing as she had no children of her own. Her contract was only to clean the house, but she also did his washing, ironing and cooked for him occasionally, and in return, he had become her handyman, helping with any maintenance work.

Marcy and her late husband were born and raised in the village. They were childhood sweethearts and even when Marcy had worked away as a nurse in her early teens, they stayed true to each other. She was twenty when she returned, and they'd got married straight away. For over thirty years they worked and lived in a small haberdashery shop and had many happy years together until cancer had taken him ten years ago, she nursed him tirelessly throughout his illness, and he died in her arms at home. After his death, she sold the property and moved into the cottage and 5 months later she found the job with Ray, she missed her husband every single day but being Ray's housekeeper filled some of the loss and sadness inside her.

As she put her key in the front door, she wondered why Ray had not mentioned that he would be home late. They usually had a little natter in the evening, he must have had some unexpected problem at work she decided. As soon as she walked into the hallway Charlie her bull mastiff dog jumped up at her with his tail wagging away, excited to see her. He was such a big dog, but as soft as a kitten, coming home to Charlie was much better than coming home to an empty house, and she gave him a loving stroke.

(Ray had gotten Charlie as a puppy, off a work colleague five years, he was sure it would make her a great companion to Marcy, and he was right, she loved the dog immediately) She hung her coat up, Charlie gave a low husky bark," I am coming," she said and followed the dog into the kitchen. Charlie sat down in front of the food cupboard, with his tail wagging. "Who's a clever boy?" she asked, and then patted his head and gave him his dog biscuit as a treat.

Ray kicked off his shoes in the hallway and immediately noticed the fresh flowers Marcy had put in a vase on the coffee table, he smiled. It felt good to be home.

The police were still at the car crash scene; they'd been there for a few hours now. "There's nothing else we can do here tonight it's getting dark, we'll start again at first light, so let's get this car off the road and back to the station." Sergeant Thomas Johnson shouted.

8.15pm and Ray had settled down to read a book then a woman's scream pierced the silence. He jumped up from his seat, then something banged against his kitchen window with force. He rushed into the kitchen, the scream had stopped, but his window had a long crack in it and his security light in the garden was lit. He grabbed his coat and dashed outside and below the window was a suitcase with its contents were strewn around the floor? He scanned the immediate area but saw nothing, he picked the case up, gathered its items, and put them behind the kitchen door. Then he took hold of his torch and returned to the garden, he walked around slowly holding the beam high, but nothing showed itself., he made his way further to the back where his swimming pool was, all the time playing the torch light from side to side then he saw something lay still beside the pool, he rushed over, he checked her pulse, it was strong. Laura was soaking wet; he slipped his arms underneath her and carefully picked her up. Then carried her into the house, placed her on the sofa and dashed upstairs to get some clothing. When he returned, she was still lifeless, he covered her with a soft woollen blanket, then moved some of wet hair that was covering her face, she opened her eyes at his touch. Her vision was blurred, she was dazed and confused and stared at him, she couldn't make out if he was a man or a woman. Ray smiled, and gradually his image became clear. The memory of being lost in the cold, dark woods flooded her, and a look of sheer horror distorted her face. Ray immediately reassured her.

"Hey, there's no need to be scared, you fell over in my garden, I heard you scream and you're safe now. Is there anybody else out there?" he asked. Laura stared blankly at him, then looked at her surroundings., yes, thank God, she was out of those dreadful woods.

"No one else, I was alone and thank you." She replied. She was tired, weak, but grateful to be in the warmth.

"You are lucky you nearly fell into my pool, you were inches away from it, you need to get out of those wet clothes before hypothermia sets in." he said and put some of his clothes for her to change into on the end of the sofa. Laura took hold of them, then remembered her suitcase.

"My case, I had a suitcase?" she said. Ray told her not to worry and that he'd found it, but all her items were soaked. Laura gave a small smile; she was freezing, but thankful, she held onto his dry garments as if they were bars of gold, and although this man seemed nice, after a rest she would leave his house, before he started asking questions. Ray looked at her and even though she looked as if she'd been dragged through a hedge backwards, he thought she was the most beautiful lady he had ever laid eyes on.

Her vanity case was undamaged, and he passed it to her. "Here, you will need this too" he said. Laura took it and for a second their hands touched, his skin was warm and soft against her cold and shaking hand. "Thank you" she quietly said. "No problem, are you hurt anywhere, do you need a doctor?" he asked. Laura told him that she was fine, then he asked if she wanted to take a warm bath, she politely declined. She didn't feel comfortable with the idea of having a bath in this stranger's house, then he suggested a shower, telling her the hot water would make her feel better. She was freezing cold and exhausted but needed to get changed, he walked her to the downstairs shower room at the back of the kitchen and as she closed the door behind her, he wondered why she was roaming about out there, alone and in the dark?

Laura looked in the mirror, she couldn't believe the state she was in, she felt terrible and looked even worse. It took ages to pick all the dirty twigs out of her hair. She stayed in the shower for a good while, washing her body repeatedly. It felt lovely to be clean again, and some warmth was brought back to her body. She dried off and then dressed in the pyjamas and dressing gown Ray had given her. She looked a funny sight in his over-sized clothes, it felt like she was being hugged by a big soft fluffy bear in his fleece dressing gown, but she was ever so grateful to feel warm again.

Ray stood by the cooker. "My housekeeper has made some lovely chicken broth soup, and always makes a large pan and far too much than I can eat, would you like some?" he asked. Laura's stomach rumbled, "Yes, thank you it sounds divine," she replied. Ray smiled "would you, like a hot drink?" she nodded and told him a green tea would be nice, then she walked into the living area and immediately noticed the sofa had been cleaned; all the mud was gone. It looked so appealing she was exhausted, she wanted to lie down, close her eyes and fall into a deep sleep. However, she needed to dry her hair first, she didn't want the cold to set back in. She knelt on a black sheepskin rug in front of the coal fire and brushed through her hair, then her thoughts went to Kay.

Kay was twenty-three years old when she walked confidently into Bret's nightclub, 'Sins', six years ago looking for work. Her blonde curls, big blue eyes, and wide smile made others smile in return. She was well spoken and immediately offered a job.

Over the years Bret had made it clear to staff, if they got too close to Laura, he would not be happy. So, they kept a distance, thinking he was just being overprotective, only Laura knew how deep Bret's insecurities really were becoming. Within a year, Kay had managed to become Laura's friend without stepping on Bret's toes. She was witty, funny, clever, and had a natural way of making Laura laugh, their friendship grew closer and Kay become a shoulder for Laura to lean on. Before the Nightclub, at aged 16, Kay married Karl Shearer a man from the village she was born and raised in. He was a police officer just like her father.

Kay had dreamed of traveling the world after school, but her parents pushed her into becoming Karl's wife, and to make them happy she agreed, she didn't love her husband and as time went on began to loathe him. He was a corrupt officer, who the whole village thought was a saint.

Kay had shared with Laura stories about his part in drug-dealing,

Destiny Rose

fraud and that her own father was no better, she knew about his corruption and was made to put up and shut up. Raised as the only child in the house, with her mother believing that the man of the house was to have the utmost respect and his word no matter what, was always final. Kay didn't want to live the same kind of life as her mother, whose main worry was keeping up appearances within the neighbourhood and trying to impress others, just so they could have dinner with the local so-called elite. Kay wanted to be equal to her husband and fought hard against Karl's domineering character. When he raised his voice to her she would answer him back, neither of them would back down. Karl had raised his hand to her and hit her many times, and she would always retaliate by picking up a heavy object and was prepared to throw it at him if he didn't stop, he knew she would follow the threat through, and would leave the house.

There was neither laughter nor smiles in her life and even though her parents knew about her husband's treatment towards her, they wouldn't hear a bad word said about him. Her life as a wife was empty and lonely, she stayed with him for eight years, then filed for divorce. Karl made sure she never received a penny from their savings which they'd both earned over the years. Her parents called her a disgrace for walking out on her marriage and were full of shame. Kay felt free when she left her hometown, and for the first time in years she smiled.)

Kay had told Laura not to worry about anything and tomorrow would be 20 days since Laure left the City, maybe Bret had accepted the fact she'd left him and perhaps everything back there was fine? And with that thought, Laura closed her eyes and continued drying her hair by the fire.

CHAPTER TWO --- DEMINICK CITY

Bret David wouldn't accept that Laura had left him. Today was the 18th day without her. He thought she would have come home by now. They had talked the morning after 'that night' and to him everything seemed fine, he explained to her his mistake in thinking she was getting too friendly with an associate, he thought she understood. Bret and his best friend Martin Darnel were in Bret's office.

"Talk to her again Martin, tell that bitch she's made her point, but my patience is wearing thin. I want to know where Laura is, and I want to know now" Bret demanded, slamming his fist on the desk. Martin sighed; even though they were best friends, Bret could be hard to cope with sometimes. It was taking a lot of patience for Martin not to shout back at him, but if he retaliated too hastily, he would end up feeling guilty and immediately see the five-year old boy who'd needed his help so many years ago. When they first met in Allonywood children's home, when Martin was eight and Bret was five.

"You really need to calm down Bret, no-one can be sure she isn't coming back to you, I know it's been a few days now, but maybe she's just..." and before Martin had time to utter another word Bret screamed:

"CALM DOWN? I WONT CALM DOWN MARTIN! And YES, I am sure she ISN'T coming BACK, and if she thinks she can leave me then she has another thing coming. Now I suggest you go and talk to that bitch of a friend of hers again because, if you don't, then I will, and I promise you it won't be very nice." With that said, Bret punched hard into the wall beside him. Martin was neither fazed nor surprised by Bret's outburst. In fact, nothing about Bret could surprise him, but this was the worst he'd ever seen his anger. Martin knew that no matter what, he would always try to help him. "Okay, but try and relax a little, we'll sort this mess out, getting yourself into a state is not going to help you; it'll just make you ill." Martin said, then he left the room. He knew it was going to be a rough road until they got Laura back, he wasn't sure she would even come back when they eventually caught up with her. The only thing he knew for sure was that he would be there for Bret every step of the way.

Kay sat happily drinking a glass of sherry, when there was a knock at her apartment door. She looked through the peephole and saw Martin standing in the hall. 'Not again, how many times do they need telling' she moaned. Then gave her nightdress a quick glance over to make sure she was decent and opened the door. She smiled then joked "Hi big boy, what brings you over here once again, are you going to tie me down to a chair this time and shine a bright light in my eyes for as much information as you can get?" and she winked at him. Martin didn't reply; instead he pushed past her and walked into the room. "Don't mess around with me Kay" he snapped, giving her a cold, hard stare. Kay had never seen Martin this angry before and was certain that his eyes had turned from a nice shade of hazel to black within seconds, and she giggled. "Good gracious Martin, you'll burst out of your clothes in a minute if you don't calm down." Martin raised his voice "This isn't a joke Kay, Bret is furious" and she was quick to reply, "oh, you mean Bret the Brat?" Martin wasn't in the mood for her attitude and grabbed her arms and glared at her, he wanted to shout but didn't, "What is wrong with you Kay? You're not stupid, you know that Bret isn't somebody you can just mess about with and playing around with me isn't going to help you either, so pack it in," he ordered. He loosened his grip, "For your own sake, just tell me where she is, there is only so much I can do for you; he'll do more than sack you if you carry on like this!" Kay caught the seriousness in Martin's voice and the sincerity in his eyes, she loved her job and was lucky to have the largest apartment above the club and didn't want to get sacked, she knew that she would have to be careful right now. "Martin, I don't know anything, I really don't. I have no idea, but Bret won't believe anything I say. Laura was unhappy and couldn't take Bret's insecurities anymore, she told me that when she was settled somewhere new, she would get in touch., and I will you tell where she is, I promise" she calmly said. Martin believed her and said.

"I will convince Bret that you don't know where she is. Just try and avoid him right now, okay?" he said. "I promise, I will stay out of his way." "Good girl," Martin said, and he gave a half smile then continued, "I know how determined Bret can be when he wants something, and Laura is something he wants, and it isn't going to be pleasant around here, not until she is back." Kay interrupted him and defiantly said. "But she isn't a piece of meat that he can own though Martin, she is a human being with feelings." Martin stared hard at her.

"I know that Kay, but that's her problem, not yours, she married him so must have known what he was like, she has to somehow try and sort this out with him. I am just trying to look out for you, I don't want to see you getting the backlash for all this." Kay was gob-smacked by his words and the sincerity in his voice over her welfare"I will stay out of his way, and I won't say anything sassy to him Martin." "That's my girl," he said then sat down on the sofa and patted the seat next to him, "come and sit down for a minute Kay" Kay sat beside him. He surprised her by saying, "I hate raising my voice to you" then he took hold of her hand, "You just concentrate on making sure you look as beautiful as ever for that stage tonight young lady." Kay smiled, Martin was only two years older than her, but it was endearing that he called her a young lady. She thanked him for looking out

Destiny Rose

for her well-being. "Hey, it's fine, I look out for all my ladies, you know that, and besides, if I'm keeping an extra eye on you, then I know no other guy is trying to move in on my special lady?" he said. "Yeah, yeah," Kay replied and grinned, dismissing Martin's compliment as a simple joke. However, he wasn't joking. He'd been attracted to Kay, since the first day she walked into the club looking for work. Her blonde hair and baby blue eyes had captivated him and over the years her sense of humour, always made him chuckle. She was always happy and confident, which appealed to him even more but, her quick wit had nearly landed her in trouble a few times with some of the male customers. Some of them were desperate to chat to her one to one and Martin had always made sure the security staff stepped in straight away, explaining to her job was to perform on the stage only.

Kay studied him closely. "You're a good man Martin Darnel and we all appreciate what you do for us. Why do you think we're all still here after all these years?" she told him. "I'm worried for you, and for Bret too, I have to convince him that you don't know anything about Laura's whereabouts. He's like a man possessed right now," Martin said.

They were still sitting side by side on the sofa, and then she softly put her hand on his leg and leant into him then gave him a little kiss on the cheek. "Thank you for caring Martin, and I wish you luck taming the tiger downstairs." she said. Then before she could take her hand from his leg, he swiftly slipped his arm around her waist and pulled her closer towards him. He looked deep into her beautiful blue eyes and whispered in her ear. "Just tell me again you will stay out of his way for the next few days?" Kay suddenly felt frozen, his breath felt heavy on her cheek, and his arm strong around her tiny waist. He was so close, much closer than he'd ever been before, she could hear his heart beating, a deep, strong, and fast beat and then suddenly she felt like her mind had been put into a trance, she took a deep breath and then quietly said, "I will Martin. I promise you I will." Martin loosened his hold on her, "I just don't want to see you get hurt." Kay was touched by Martin's softness, she gazed into his eyes and for a moment they stared at each other. She felt confused by the feelings her body was experiencing. She had never realised until now, how strong and caring he was.

"I'm sorry that you're involved in all this too, Martin," she said.

"Kay, I've always been involved in Bret's life, and always will be no matter what," he quietly said and added, " And I would like to be there for you too Kay" Then he went quiet, he released his hold on her and stood up. "Now I'm going to sort this mess out, I will see you later" he said. Kay watched him walk over to the apartment door expecting him to leave right away, but as he reached it, he stopped and turned around to look at her, and instead of leaving he walked back over to the sofa and taking hold of her hands, gently he pulled her onto her feet. He cupped her face with his strong hands and kissed her gently on the cheek.

"Don't forget your promise to me," he said.

"I promise," she replied. Kay was back in that trance-like state and she watched him leave the apartment. She didn't move an inch and stood still feeling totally bewildered by what had just happened between them. Whatever it was, it sure felt nice…

Kay knew a little bit of information about Laura's movements, but she wouldn't tell anybody anything, especially Bret and was sure that Martin could calm Bret down; then she wondered what it was between the two men that had made them so close. They were so very different. Bret could be stubborn, loud and mean, whilst Martin was calm and patient, but nothing seemed to unsettle their friendship. Her thoughts then went to Laura and hoped she was okay. Bret was going to be hard work over the next few days and she would have to walk on eggshells around him. Tonight, was her solo dance act on stage and she wasn't looking forward to it, at all.

Martin was in Bret's office retelling the conversation with Kay, and Bret interrupted him mid-sentence.
"What do you mean she doesn't know anything? Of course, she does, the lying scheming bitch. She probably knows everything the slut, I'm going over there right now, I've had enough of that smart-mouthed tart. I will kill the whore if she doesn't tell me where Laura is." Bret stood up from his chair, but Martin put his hands calmly but firmly on his friend's shoulders, stopping him from moving.
"I'm telling you Bret; she doesn't know anything. Laura must have wanted it that way, she knew Kay would be the first person you'd go to for answers, so she made sure she knew nothing. She wanted to disappear quietly and that is exactly what she has done." Bret was furious, he could feel rage filling him and stared angrily at Martin. Martin was 31 and only a couple of years older than Bret, he was 6 ft. 3 and seemed to tower Bret's 5 ft. 9. If Martin wanted to overpower him, they both knew he could do it easily. Martin gave his friend a hard stare in reply. Then Bret bowed his head down low and quietly said. "How could she do this, why did she do this, I gave her everything the ungrateful bitch, she didn't have to leave me; we could have worked it out?" Martin could see the despair in his friend's face.
"Try to relax a little Bret, she really isn't worth getting this upset over, no woman is," he said. Bret calmly walked over to the window and looked out onto the street below. It was a quiet street considering their club was in the middle of the city centre, but it was a one-way system, which kept traffic low. Plus, there were no clothes shops here; it was mostly office buildings so that kept pedestrian numbers down.

Destiny Rose

Bret stared outside, Martin's words swirled around in his head, he turned around and said, "No Martin, you are wrong. She is worth it, oh yes, she is. She belongs to me and she should be here with me, and I'm going to find her." Martin was watching his friend falling apart before his eyes, and there was nothing he could do, but to be there to help him get through this storm.

Martin had always been there for Bret and always would be, at the age of sixteen he could legally leave the care home, which he did, but he stayed local, finding work and lodgings. Bret left two years later, and they made their way to the City which was more than 300 miles away from the home. The further away the better... They shared accommodation in the city, and it wasn't long before they were buying and selling used cars. Spare money was saved and before long they'd bought a rundown house which they restored and sold on, making a healthy profit. Their next purchase was a public house, they both had their own flats by now. The pub soon became known for streaming live sports and occasionally catering for a small boxing match in the space above the pub. They bought another pub and for a good price on the outskirts of the city, which was a quieter place with a countryside setting. It had a large log fire in the main room with oak beams on the ceilings. Both pubs ran smoothly and were successful. Bret was nineteen when they bought their nightclub which they called 'Sins' It was in the heart of the city.

They both lived a short walk away in top-floor apartments in a modern tower block overlooking the city. Over the years the club had become known as a gentleman's club and even though ladies were more than welcome none ever came in. The club attracted more female workers than male, and so it had become what it was today, with female exotic dancing acts on the stage at weekends. The accommodation above was there for staff that needed it. It was highly respected place and catered for businessmen, police officers; and all sorts of clientele. The main room was large and of modern design, with highly polished oversize ceramic floor tiles in black and white. The bar ran the full length of one side of the room and was made of steel and smoked glass. Large black and white pictures hung on the walls, lights above each one to shine on the image. The pictures were of film-stars from the past: Mary Pickford, Mae West, Vivien Leigh and Humphrey Bogart was the only male picture. The stage was circular and built up on golden steps. The lighting and décor gave the club a 1950s feeling. There was a door behind the stage leading to a large dressing room making it easy for the acts to enter without having to walk amongst the audience. Card games and business deals would go on in the club, but they'd be kept out of view, being conducted in the back rooms with full waiter/waitress service provided. Bret and Martin worked very hard keeping their customers and associates happy. Martin was the thinker and planner, as well as being the one who calmed Bret down after he had bitten off more than he could chew. He could lose his temper fast, so Martin would step in rather than lose a deal. They were friends as well as business partners, and it worked out well for them both

Bret stared helplessly at Martin; "You have to help me. I've checked all her credit cards, rung the phone company - she hasn't used her cards or made a call. I just don't know what else to do?" Martin looked at him, his expression was one of fear. It was the same look Martin had seen on Bret's face a few times and he said.

"Listen here is what we will do, we'll find out how she's travelling so we can then get some idea of which way she's heading. How does that sound?" Bret nodded, "Yeah, that sounds good to me, I'll ring Jake and Ron and get them to show her picture around, to try and get some info." "Okay, you do

Destiny Rose

that." Martin replied. "I'll go and speak to the staff and make sure that everything's on time for tonight's show." Martin felt sure that when they caught up with Laura, she wouldn't want to come back and he was worried how Bret would take that, but he would have to accept it, there would be nothing either of them could do about it. He made his way to the lobby where some of the staff were talking. Frankie, Lucy, and Hannah were standing near the entrance desk, none of the staff mentioned Bret's low mood over the last few days they just all got on with their jobs. They filled Martin in on the schedule for the evening. Bret had shown little interest in the club over the last few days, so Martin was thankful they were all on top of things.

Destiny Rose

CHAPTER THREE --- THE TRUTH

Laura was still drying her hair by the fire when Ray came out of the kitchen carrying a tray with soup and hot drinks. He passed Laura two paracetamol and a glass of water.

"Take them before you eat - they'll help get your temperature down. He settled into his chair and watched her brush her hair. It looked like strands of silk draping down her back and resting on her hips. Then his thoughts went to her family,

"Your husband must be frantic with worry, you should ring your family and let them know you are okay and where you are" he said. His words took Laura by surprise, she looked at him and it was only then that she noticed she was still wearing her wedding ring.

Her mind went into a spin, why on earth did she still have his ring on her finger, she should have left it behind, but it hadn't even crossed her mind to take it off. You stupid, stupid woman, her mind cried.... Being married was the only thing she wanted to forget, and here she was still wearing his ring.

She began panicking: what if she had forgotten something else, something more important than the ring, what if Bret was on his way here right now, what would she say to him, and what would he do to this man if he sees him helping her?... Worries and fears spun around her mind. What was she going to say to this man?

Ray sat silently watching her. she'd stopped drying her hair and was staring at the ring on her finger. He stood up and walked over to her, "Is everything okay?" he asked. He felt the nervous tension coming from her. She turned to face him, "Yes, I'm sorry, everything's fine" she replied.   Ray knelt beside her, "Do you want me to contact your husband?"   She didn't know what to say, and he noticed her distress.   Then thinking quickly, she blurted out: "Yes, yes, my family will be worried about me, but not my husband because I'm not married. I only wear this ring because I don't want to be in a relationship with anybody right now" "Well, it's a lovely ring it looks like a real diamond, and it fooled me "Ray said.

"Oh yes, it is, it has to look like the real thing, but it's only costume jewellery" she replied nervously, then went on to explain that it was a trick that many ladies played when they wanted to remain single, and not to be hassled for a date whenever they went out.   Ray smiled and said,

"so, you're playing a game of reverse psychology with people?" and he chuckled.   Laura nodded,

"Yes, I guess I am." She replied.

"Very clever, so you're not married, and you were out being social, but there's nothing social around here for miles. Did you have a mobile phone with you, why didn't you call someone for help. It's the middle of March and one of the coldest ones we've ever had?" Laura's head spun from all the questions: she was so tired, but she knew she had to do some fast thinking.

"We've only just moved into a new area - my parents retired recently wanting a quieter life and decided to move away from the city. They live in a little village not far away from here. I haven't got my bearings yet, and decided to go out for the day, I was trying to find the bus station, and got completely lost," she lied.

"Why didn't you phone for help when you got lost?" Laura said she'd lost her mobile phone in the woods.

"Why did you need a suitcase, if you'd only gone out for the day?" Laura's head started to pound, then she said, "'I had been to a friend's house early in the morning to pick some of my belongings up, and I was taking them home. "Oh, I see," he answered; he had no reason to doubt her story.

"Do they like village life?" He asked, Laura was quick to reply "Yes, they do, it's a lovely little village."

"Is it Langley or Great Oak?" he asked "Langley," she replied, then turned away from him, hoping he wouldn't notice she was telling lies. She didn't want to lie but didn't want him knowing the truth. His questions were too much for her and abruptly she stood up and announced that as soon as her clothes were dry, she would get dressed and go home. She sat down on his sofa and picked up her drink a cup of hot chocolate.

"No buses or taxis run after 8pm because it's such a quiet area, you can ring your parents and let them know you're safe, they can pick you up or I can drive you to them, it wouldn't be a problem." he said. She was so tired, but as though she'd rehearsed the lines earlier, convincingly she said: "I can't ring them because they think I'm at a friend's house, but I wasn't going to stay with a friend. I was going to see a band in the city, and I was going to stay over in a motel."

"Alone?" he quizzed.

"Yes, alone" she said wearily. She looked at him, he had kind eyes; they were a striking midnight blue and his lashes were long and dark, which made his eye colour appear brighter. His hair was short and dark, and his strong jawline finished his appearance off perfectly. He was a handsome man; she guessed his age at around forty; and she wondered how such a strong and fine-looking man could be so gentle and caring. She smiled at him, grateful for his help. She leant forwards to put her cup on the tray and a sharp pain stabbed into her ribs and she cried out.

"What is it?" Ray asked and knelt in front of her. The pain felt as if a knife was piercing its way through her ribs to her heart. "I don't know?" she replied. "You must have hurt yourself when you fell, let me look at it," he said. She eased herself down on

Destiny Rose

the sofa, and as she lay there, she wanted to fall asleep, and right at this moment she didn't care if she never woke up again.

"Can you show me where the pain is?" She took hold of his hand and slid it under the pyjama top, placing it near the top of her ribcage. Ray didn't want to press down too hard on the injury and said, "I'll have to look at it, is that okay?" Laura nodded her approval. He opened a few buttons on her top and gently removed the fabric covering her body. His eyes fixed on her perfectly formed breasts. Opening her eyes, she saw his stare she had completely forgotten she didn't have a brassiere on but was tired and in too much pain to be embarrassed, so closed her eyes.

She was beautiful. He had met many women in his life, but none of them had ever had this effect on him. Physically this lady was everything he wanted in a woman. He dragged his eyes away from her breasts and noticed the black bruise at the top of her ribcage.

"You are injured, I'll get a doctor to look at this," he said. Laura was startled at his words. She couldn't be seen by a medic. She didn't want to be questioned by anybody and she couldn't lie to this man anymore, she had to tell him the truth.

"No, please don't. I know you're only trying to help me but no doctors please." Ray looked at her, confused,

"Why not, I don't understand, we don't know what's happened here, you could have broken ribs. I must call a doctor. However, as he was about to move away Laura reached out her hand and tugged on the leg of his trousers.

"I know what is wrong with me," she said. He knelt on the floor again. "Are you positive that you know what's wrong with you?" he asked.

"Yes, I am, please believe me, I will explain everything" Ray buttoned her pyjama top back up, then he covered her with a warm blanket, and Laura began to cry. He put his arm around her hoping it would bring her some comfort but, the tears didn't stop. She was utterly exhausted, the lack of sleep and food over the last few days, the dire situation she was in, plus Ray's questions had taken their toll. She held onto his arm and cried; he kept his arm around her until she became calm again. She felt safe with his strong arm around her. She wanted to feel safe and secure forever. She had never felt such comfort from a man before and her mind wondered why she couldn't have met somebody like this stranger before, instead of a jealous brute like her husband. When Laura had calmed down, she looked at Ray and said, "I'm sorry, I've lied to you" and went on to tell him everything about how she'd ended up in Little Hampton and how the bruise on her chest was a cracked rib that she'd received when her husband had pushed her up against a wall. Her eyes never left his and then she quietly said,

"I'm so sorry." The shame of lying to him filled her, and her tears started again.

"Hey, it's okay, don't cry," Ray said, reassuring her and gently cupping her face in his hands. He could see she was exhausted and scared and continued, "We can call a doctor first thing in the morning, right now, you need a good sleep." She looked at him,

"I never meant to fall into your garden."

"It's okay, I'm glad I found you," and without thinking he gently stroked her hair. "You've done nothing wrong and I'm happy you found your way into my garden. Although the weather, the timing, and the reason could have been much better," he said in a jovial way. Laura responded by smiling.

"There's more I need to tell you. You know nothing about me, and I need to be honest with you" she said. Laura felt that, unless she told this man everything, then she was betraying him in some way. She needed him to know her story because he seemed such a caring man, and he needed to know just what kind of trouble she could be bringing into his life merely by falling into his garden.

Then she told him everything about her, starting with her time in care and about Bret, explaining he had been brought up in care too which made her feel an instant connection with him, and how she tried to help him with his insecurities, but had just gotten worse, then she said, "Maybe it's all my fault that I was put into care and maybe it was my fault that Bret behaved the way he did toward me." She fell silent, fear and anxiety creeping over her. Then he said, "Hey it's okay, just stay calm, none of it is your fault, we cannot control who we are born to or who we meet in life, we must stay strong and cope with whatever life brings to us. Your husband is responsible for his own actions and not you. I often wonder why women don't just leave the first time a man becomes abusive" almost questioningly.

Laura told him that Bret's anger problems hadn't shown up until two years of living together. Over the years she'd tried to work his temper out by helping him gain control and stopping his angry outbursts, but she would have had to be a mind reader to understand his emotions which set the behaviour off. Then she told Ray about Kay and how they'd conspired together so she could leave him. Ray went silent, stunned at the thought of a woman living with a possessive and angry man for over ten years and still trying to help him so he could live a better way of life.

They were both in deep thought. She had never felt comfortable talking to anyone other than Kay about her life with Bret, but she felt that she'd had no choice but to tell this man.

"Stay here tonight as my guest, please, and I will get my doctor first thing in the morning. 100% discretion; I assure you". Laura desperately needed to sleep. "Yes, I will stay, thank you," she replied. "Don't be worrying about anything other than getting a good sleep," he said. She smiled, closed her eyes and immediately fell asleep. Ray watched her as she slept; she was beautiful, he couldn't imagine anybody wanting to hurt her. Anger and contempt for a man he didn't even know filled him, but, one thing was certain, if Bret David ever crossed his path, he'd better tread carefully. Bret wasn't a man in his eyes, he was a coward and a bully, and while this lady was staying under his roof, he would look after her. Then he bent down and gently kissed her on the forehead.

Destiny Rose

CHAPTER FOUR ---THE PLAN

Back in Deminick, the week had gone as well as it could have. Bret and Martin's search for Laura would begin today. Kay had stayed out of Bret's way, and kept her distance from Martin too; she didn't want to give Bret another reason to get angry with her.

Martin's alarm woke him up at 8am. He stretched and let out a big yawn. He knew the next few days were going to be tiring. Bret had been up since 6 am; the information he'd been waiting for had come through late last night. An HGV driver had seen Laura, she was driving a silver car leaving a petrol station in Cedar Hill a village over 300 miles away. That would be their destination and Bret was hoping the petrol station had CCTV cameras, at least he had something which was better than nothing. He had showered and was examining his image in the bathroom mirror. He looked pale and thin; it was no wonder because he hadn't slept properly without Laura. His brown eyes looked black and sunken and he had dark rings underneath them. Water dripped from his short curly dark hair. His lack of personal grooming had left him with a week-old growth of facial hair. Why has she done this? why did she have to leave me? She could have stayed with me. She SHOULD have stayed with me, his mind shouted out. Tears filled his eyes, but he didn't cry he wouldn't cry for anyone. He stared deeply at his reflection and he saw the truth in his eyes. He knew exactly why she left him; his behaviour had been too much for her.

He bowed his head down low, 'you can change, you will change if you try hard enough' he told him-self, but deep down he knew he couldn't. Then he wondered why he'd allowed himself to get so close to her; he'd never fallen in love before. He was okay living as a single person with a one-night stand here and there. He never should have put his heart and mind in a position where they'd become weak, and now he couldn't control his feelings and anger. He tried many times to stop himself from raging at his wife, but he couldn't control it. The anger would build up, and then rage erupted like a volcano. He felt disgusted and ashamed that the kindest and sincerest person he'd ever met was to be the one to suffer the most because of who he'd become.

'During childhood Bret had built a wall around his heart and his mind - and as he got older his only concern was for money and business. They were the most important things in his life, until Laura had come along, and his world had changed forever'

Bret held his shaver to his face. He didn't want to think about the bad parts of his relationship with Laura - there had been many good times as well as bad, and he would have to think about those. He had to concentrate on them. He started to shave the thick hair from his face.

'Bret had been blocking feelings out ever since the first time in the children's home when an evil man hurt him. He never knew his parents and was raised by his grandmother for the first two years of his life and when she'd passed away, he was sent to the home. He was five when the abuse had begun. Bret was scared to death of Mr. Surringer, the head of the home and he told Bret that if he ever told anybody what he was doing to him he would kill him. All the children did as they were told they lived in fear. The abuse Bret suffered carried on for a year until the day Martin Darnell walked into his life. Martin was 7 years old when Bret met him and tall for his age. He lost his parents in a car crash

Destiny Rose

when he was 4 and went to live with his Grand-Mother until ill health left her with no choice but to put him into the care system.

Allonywood Children's Home was for boys was an old building with four floors. No more than thirty children lived there at one time. The first level was for lessons and eating meals. The second level had two dorms with beds in, those who were ten years and older stayed in a separate dorm from the younger ones and the whole of the top floor of the building was the headmaster of the house, Mr. Surringer's office and nobody went up there unless ordered to do so. Wardens controlled the home, they were strict teachers, with more females than males. The place was run on a timetable, the over-tens played outside first and then had lessons, the younger children had the reverse schedule. The Rota kept the home in order and the children, regardless of age were taught independence quickly. They'd make their own beds and as neat as possible. Clothes, lesson books, and play items had to be cleaned and cared for by each child. If any of the children slacked in tidiness, they'd get a ruler on the knuckles or whipped with a strap on the palms of their hands. Children who continued to slack or who were disobedient would get the cane across the back of their bare legs.

Martin had been in the home for around two months, but neither he nor Bret's paths had crossed until a day that neither of them would ever forget. Morning lessons had just finished his morning lesson when Martins teacher asked him to take a letter to the headmaster's office. "And don't dilly or dally along your way, I will be waiting for your return" she added. Martin took the envelope; the other children were glad they hadn't been chosen. The only way to get to the top floor was on an old rickety iron spiral staircase. There was a wider staircase in the

Destiny Rose

middle of the home, but it only went up to the third floor. Some of the children played a game on the staircase, they would dare each other to see who could get to the top in the fastest time. The higher they got the darker it became and, they'd end up running back down not even making it half-way. The children who did manage to make it to the top were instantly seen as being brave, a status that many children wanted to share.

This was the first-time Martin had gone up the staircase and when he reached the top he was met with a long, dark, and narrow corridor. There was no windows or light, just a long dark tunnel and at the end was a large wooden door. Although it was dark, and more than a little frightening Martin was a brave lad; he confidently strode to the door. He ignored the 'DO NOT DISTURB' sign hanging on the knob, turned the handle and walked straight in. Martin stopped dead in his tracks at the sight he saw. The pale face of a petrified boy younger than himself looked at him, with fear in his eyes. he was terrified, and tears streamed down his cheeks, the image would stay with him forever. The child was standing at the side of the head of the home who was sitting on his chair behind his desk. Martin didn't know why the boy was half undressed, or why he was crying, but he knew something was very wrong. The atmosphere in the room was chilling, then the headmaster looked at Martin and shouted angrily,

"What do you want little runt?" Martin had never seen the man before he looked at Martin trembling boy. "What's he doing, is he hurting you?" The lad nodded. Martin looked at the headmaster, he wasn't scared of him and he ran at the man, punching and kicking him hard in his legs. The man went to slap Martins across the face, but Martins grabbed his wrist and stopped him. "Leave him alone, you are hurting him, you won't hurt him again, leave him alone, do you hear me? Martin screamed out. Bret quickly picked up his clothes and got dressed. Mr. Surringer grabbed Martin by his shoulder and held him tight. "How dare you, insolent little rat, I'll have you on locked up for a week," he seethed, but Martin didn't stop and continued to kick and punch out at him, "You do that Mr, and I'll tell everybody you were hurting him, they may not be able to see me if you have me locked away, but they will hear me when I shout!" Martin shouted out in rage. Surringer let go of him and shoved him away. "Listen hear the pair of you, his punishment for being insolent is over now and you both can leave, but, before you go remember this: I can have the pair of you shipped out of here and taken far away. Separate you to different countries where nobody will understand your language. So, let this be the last we hear of this today. It's over now, there'll be no more punishment for him be on your way the pair of you," Martin put his arm around Bret's shoulder and together they made their way back down the staircase. Martin made a promise to Bret, he swore that no one would ever hurt him again, not if he could help it.

They were too scared to tell anyone about Surringer, in case they got shipped off to only God knows where? They became as close as brothers and kept the abuse Bret suffered a secret

Bret knew that he couldn't turn the clock back to change what had happened, but with Martin's friendship he had learnt to cope. He'd always found relationships with anyone other than Martin challenging, and so he'd learnt to keep an emotional distance from others. He'd accepted that what had happened to him all those years ago and the memories would stay with him forever but what he couldn't accept, was that Laura had left him.

Bret, now clean-shaven, suddenly thought 'what if Laura has met another man - maybe that's why she left?' The thought slowly took root and then came anger. He couldn't stand the thought of another man holding Laura, another man loving her: she

Destiny Rose

belonged to him. He trembled with rage and clenching his fist he punched the mirror in front of him. Blood dripped freely from his knuckles, but he didn't care. His mind was focused on Laura. She knew exactly what he was like when she met him. He'd explained how insecure he was, and no matter what, she was going to come back home with him.

Martin was eating his breakfast when Bret rang. Today was the day he and Bret had decided to call a meeting with the staff to make plans for the club while they were away for a few days.

"Yes, everything is on schedule, I will see you downstairs soon" Martin said and hung the phone up then he rang Kay to inform her of the meeting. Kays heart skipped a beat when he told her he didn't like leaving her. To her ears it sounded as though he would miss only her and not the other girls. "Don't worry, I will be okay Martin, I promise." she told him.

"Yes I know you will, because I've asked Ron to keep an extra eye on you, just in case you get any trouble from any of the guests, so you must ring him right away if you need anything while I'm gone?" "Of course, I will, and thank you" she said. Martin was making her feel very special indeed, and she liked it.

"Okay, I'll see you downstairs later," he finished. Kay put the receiver down and smiled. Her heart was thumping with excitement by his words.

Martin wondered why he suddenly wanted to express his concern for Kay. He'd kept it hidden for years, but now he wanted to tell her, and he couldn't work out why. The only thing he could think of was seeing Bret so angry at her, had made him realise how much he really did care for her. He had never had a long relationship with a woman before, he had dated many ladies, but never felt the way he felt about Kay. He would be honest with her and tell her exactly how he felt the next time he saw her, he had nothing to lose, she could only say no. It was now 10am. Bret and Martin were sat in the main room waiting for the staff to arrive for the meeting. Both men were in deep thought; Bret looked around the room and his eyes stopped at the empty bar and his thoughts went back to the time that he'd first seen Laura. He was sat chatting to customers and hadn't been able to take his eyes off her; she was carrying a tray of drinks to the table beside his. Her long dark hair swayed gently around her hips and she caught him looking at her. Their eyes locked, and she smiled. She was beautiful and from that moment he was hooked. As she got closer to the table, he noticed her hands trembling, the weight of the tray was too heavy for her. He stood up, took the tray from her hands and placed it down on the table next to his. She didn't know who he was, and she thanked him. "No need to thank me, try fewer drinks next time," he said. He watched her discreetly while she worked. It was obvious she was new to bar-work, because the bartenders were showing her how to pour the simplest of spirits into the correct glasses in the correct manner. He laughed when he saw her trying to stop the flow of alcohol from the pumps at the right time, she laughed and smiled all evening. She possessed a natural innocence, which made Bret wonder why such a sweet-looking lady would want to work in a busy nightclub. She didn't act like the usual girls who came into the club looking for employment.

Later that evening, Bret introduced himself to Laura, and on her break, they talked and laughed for a while. Laura told him that she'd never drunk a cocktail before, and creating one was a task! She had never been into a nightclub before either until she'd come into this one, and the only reason she'd applied for the job was because of the accommodation which came with it.

Bret knew after that first night of talking with her, that he wanted her, and after that evening the more, he saw of her the more he desired her. Then his thoughts and memories were

Destiny Rose

broken by Ron's bellowing voice... "What's going on boss, where is everybody?" Bret looked at him, and said, "We'll tell you everything when everyone is here, so I don't have to keep repeating myself, if that's okay?" "Of course, I know you're not a parrot, all they do is repeat-repeat-repeat" Ron joked, and he sat down. Bret smiled and replied, "you are starting to sound like a frog with all that repeating!" they all laughed. Then Dale the bar manager entered the room followed by security man Jake. Not long afterwards came Archie the head chef. Diane the head waitress, then Lucy and Hannah who over-saw the stage, and the last one in was Frankie; he took care of accounts for the card games and the back-room business deals. Bret didn't waste any time informing them that he and Martin were leaving today for a business trip. He told them they could be back within days or even a week or two, and he and Martin were putting their trust in them to keep things running as smooth as usual. He looked at each person, "Do any of you have questions?" he asked. No-one had any questions then Frankie said, "We've been doing this job long enough now, so have no fear" he said, laughing heartily.

"Thanks pal," Bret replied. Everyone seemed to know exactly what they'd be doing over the coming weeks. Then Martin said

"Extra pay will go to you all at the end of the month for helping us out at such short notice." The staff read the agenda sheets and then Martin stood up. "Bret can we have a private word please?" Bret looked puzzled. "Sure," and they walked over to the bar and Martin said, "a week or two? You never said anything about weeks?" Bret was still puzzled.

"We have to be realistic Martin; we should add time for the unexpected. Anyway, look at it as if we're taking a short holiday, I mean there's nothing here for you to rush back to, is there?" Then the door beside the bar slammed shut, startling both men and Kay was standing there. She stayed silent. Martin gave her a smile. "No, there's no reason to rush back, I just wasn't expecting to be away for weeks, perhaps one week at the most." Then Bret said, "can we just get this meeting over, so we can pack and head off please?" and he walked back to his seat. Martin walked over to Kay. "Hi, are you okay?" he asked. "Yes, I'm fine - and you?"

"Couldn't be better," Martin replied, a hint of sarcasm colouring his voice. He was happy to see Kay, but he was feeling frustrated and uncertain how Bret's problem with Laura was going to end, or even how long it would take find her... "I'm sorry Kay, ignore my mood - everything really is okay," and he gave her a little smile. Kay could see he was tired. Normally, he was full of life. She was just about to speak but Bret shouted.

"Martin, does she have to be here?" Martin gave Kay a compassionate look. Kay didn't need to be at the meeting she only came down to catch a few minutes with Martin. She turned to face Bret and calmly, but also with a sharp tone, replied,

"No Bret, I don't need to be here, I came down to see if anybody wanted any refreshment's?" and then she went silent.

"Coffee with two sugars my dear, "Ron shouted out and Jake echoed him. Bret shot Kay a look of contempt then turned away. Martin followed her into the kitchen area. "We could be away for a week or two," he said, and watched as she prepared the drinks.

"Yes, I heard," she replied, deliberately not looking at him.

"I bet you won't even notice I'm gone," he said. She faced him, and he smiled.

"You're just teasing me Martin, you know that we'll all miss you," she said. "Maybe I am teasing you a little, but I really would like to know if just you not the other girls, would miss me?" Kay inspected him: he was a good-looking man, tall, dark, strong, and handsome. His dark brown eyes met her thoughtful look, and she said, "You won't be gone for too long I am sure of it, and I will still be here working so I won't have time to miss you." Then she turned her back and continued with the drinks.

Martin up behind her, and gently slipped his hands around her waist and rested them there, then quietly he said. "Before you pick that tray up, I need to tell you something, I can't keep it in anymore Kay." Kay froze at his words and his touch sent shivers up her spine. What was wrong with her? This was Martin her friend, why was he having this effect on her and why was he saying all this? Then her thoughts were overridden as he pushed his body closer to her. She could feel his heartbeat against her back, she was sure her heart had skipped more than a beat, and she gripped the edge of the kitchen worktop. "Kay, you are a beautiful woman," he whispered. His hands moved down from her waist to her hips and Kay's temperature rose, her legs turned to jelly, and she felt sure that any moment they would give out on her. However, she didn't collapse, and she remained standing up! She couldn't find the words for the sensations of delight filling her, his words were dancing around her mind. She'd been unprepared for what every inch of her body was experiencing right now at his touch and his words.

Martin didn't mind that Kay was silent; he was deep in the moment, holding her close, while telling her how he felt. He was glad she wasn't looking at him: it made telling her easier and still holding her, he said, "Kay, I will understand if you don't feel the same way about me, as I do about you. If you need time to think about it, take all the time you need." Kay felt as if she had drunk a bottle of sherry. His sweet words and touch, left her incapable of any rational thought and she simply said, "Yes, I agree, I do." Martin wasn't sure what she was agreeing to, but he didn't care; she had said yes, and that sent his urge for her soaring. He turned her around to face him, their eyes met, he pulled her closer. She could feel every inch of his muscular body against her own. His hand glided up her spine and caressed the nape of her neck softly. "I've waited such a long time to tell you how beautiful you are and show you how I feel." Then he kissed her. Her lips met his with an unbridled urgency and they both felt the desperate want and need for each other. Within seconds they were both lost in a wonderful, magical place that belonged to them, and nobody else. Kay felt as if she was floating, slowly they parted, and Martin gazed into her love-filled eyes.

"I want to feel every inch of you so much Kay." Kay felt his need for her, strong and hard, every inch of him told her how he felt, and she wanted to feel him too. "I feel the same Martin." She said. They held each other close, both knowing they would have to put their feelings on hold until he returned from the trip. They also knew there would be no turning back from what they were both experiencing. Neither of them had ever felt it before and they knew they wanted more. Standing in silence, they held each other. Then Jake shouted. "How long does it take you to make a few drinks; hurry up will you Kay?" Reluctantly, she pulled away from martin, finished the drinks, Martin took hold of the tray,

"I never should have left it this long; I should have said something earlier." Kay looked at him,

"It's better late than never Martin, because today could be the beginning of the rest of our lives together." Martin smiled.

At 2pm, the men were ready to set off on their journey. Martin put their luggage into the boot of the car and was just about to shut it when Bret stopped him. I've forgotten something that I need to put in there and he raced back into the club, he rushed up the stairs and into his office. From inside the bottom drawer of his desk, he took out a handgun, he made sure it was loaded before putting it into the inside pocket of a jacket that was hanging on a coat stand. Martin, Jake, Ron and Kay were talking

Destiny Rose

on the pavement outside when Bret returned. The Bret placed his jacket carefully on top of the luggage and shut the boot door. Kay looked at Martin and said. "Don't worry about us back here. You take care, and hurry back". Then Ron joked. "Him worry about us; it should be us worrying about them?" Jake laughed. Kay gave a strained smile, and immediately her mind wondered if Martin would be safe going on this journey? However, she knew Martin could handle Bret, so she wiped the doubt from her mind.

"I'll be back before you know it." Martin reassured her, and he gave Kay a playful elbow nudge and without caring who saw him he gave her a little kiss on the cheek. "Okay" she answered. The two men set off with Martin driving his limited-edition two-seater TX2 sports car.

Destiny Rose

CHAPTER FIVE --- CONNECTIONS

Today was Saturday it was 11.55am. Ray woke early but left Laura to sleep in on the sofa. She slept till midday and when she woke, she saw Ray, sitting in his armchair. He smiled,

"Remember me? I'm the one who came to your rescue in the dark hours of the night," he said, with a hint of humour. She smiled too, "Yes, I remember - I was lucky you found me when you did. I could have been out there all night," she replied, and shuddered at the thought. She was feeling much better today and even though her limbs were aching, she was sure they would recover fully over the next few days. Ray got up and went into the kitchen to make them a drink and something to eat. Considering how exhausted she had been the night before, she remembered everything. She looked around the room: tall, smooth plastered walls painted in a hint of cream. A large square grey rug covered the natural oak flooring and an oak coffee table sat on the rug. The room had minimal furniture and little décor, no pictures anywhere; the only items which gave the room some decoration were two large exotic potted plants. The fireplace was the room's centrepiece: it featured an inglenook with enough room to fit two armchairs inside. The fire itself was a cast iron stove surrounded by rustic brick. It looked charming and gave off a lot of warmth. The stairs were open plan, made of the same wood as the oak floor. She got up and went to the full-length window behind the sofa and looked at the front garden. The lawn was about two acres and well-kept. A gravel driveway led down to an iron gateway and a brick wall at least five-foot high formed the property's boundary. Ray returned with a tray, he poured them both a coffee, Laura sat down on the sofa and he handed her a drink.

Destiny Rose

"How are you feeling today?" he asked? Much better, I didn't think yesterday was ever going to end, my day just kept getting worse" she said. He smiled, then replied, "It's over now, you can recover, and do you want to know something important?" Laura's eyes widened with curiosity. "Yes, what?" she asked.

"Well, you have showered in my home, slept on my sofa, worn my clothes and I don't even know your name?" Laura was taken by surprise and giggled.

"I don't know yours either, so I guess that makes us even, my name is Laura Lee. "

"It's nice to meet you Miss Lee. My name is Raymond, Richard, Maitland, but I never get called Raymond, not unless I'm being scolded by my dear and lovely mother" and they both laughed.

This man really did have a way of making Laura feel at ease. She enjoyed her toast and coffee and after it she returned to the window. She stared outside and after a minute, turned to look at Ray. "Does the brick wall go all the way around your house?" He walked to her side, "Yes, it does, why?" Confusion crossed her face, "but, if that brick wall goes all the way around your garden then how did I end up out of those woods and inside, because I wouldn't have been able to climb that brick wall?"

"Oh right," he replied and then explained how there was a break in the wall in the back garden and that it was such a little gap just a few feet wide, and she had been lucky to find it. He explained that he had the opening put in for his housekeeper, so she could cut through to get home much quicker rather than using the longer route out front. "How thoughtful" she remarked "Thank you, you were extremely fortunate finding the break in the wall. Fate must have played a hand somewhere or maybe the Angels guided you to my garden?" She looked at Ray. "That's a sweet thing to say, but I have so much worry on my mind and Angels would certainly not pass my burdens onto anyone else. I did follow a cat though, which is what led me here." Ray looked at her with a quizzical expression. "Animals can be Angels too, and as for being a worry or a burden to others everybody has them, and sharing your worries and burdens with someone else, makes the weight a lot lighter." Laura didn't say anything; he was a wise, strong man, his words filled her with hope. Then he broke her thoughts, "the doctor is coming to look at you later. I hope that's okay?" he asked. It was fine, and she nodded her acceptance. Ray poured them both another coffee,

"How's the pain in your chest?" he asked

"It feels better, the rest has done it some good" she answered. A few seconds passed, and she said, "those woods were so dark I thought I would never get out." Ray strained a smile; "How long were you in the woods?" he asked. "Only a few hours" she replied then told him over the last couple of weeks, and about the loss of her car. "That is a mighty long time of driving you did, no wonder you were shattered" he said. Laura nodded and said. "When the doctor has seen me this evening, I' will be moving on. I can travel by train the rest of the way." Ray's thoughts immediately went to the abandoned car the police had found. He looked at her and smiled, he wasn't going to tell her that the police had found her car, he didn't want to worry or frighten her any more than she already was. Then he said.

"Don't worry about the car - it's just a damaged vehicle whose owner has simply walked away from it. You haven't hurt anybody which is the main thing, or damaged property so you won't get into any trouble." Laura looked at him, he may be right, but the police would want answers to questions, then she said, "But if they find out it was me; they'll file a report which Bret could use to find me. Besides I could have easily hurt somebody on that road last night – I was tired and fell asleep at the wheel it was the only explanation ..." Ray was a cautious driver as well as a careful one, he'd been this way all his life. He would never fall asleep at the wheel of a car and had never understood how anybody could, but this situation was complex, and he was just thankful Laura hadn't hurt or killed herself or anybody else.

"Don't beat yourself up, I'm sure you won't do it again?"

"No, never again," she replied, and he believed her. He changed the subject and told her about Marcy.

Marcy had rung earlier that morning. She had been into the village and heard the news about the abandoned car, gossip travelled fast around here. He felt there was no need to tell her about Laura, he would see her on Monday and tell her then.

The doctor came at 5 pm his visit lasted an hour. Laura's main problem was a fractured rib, and with plenty of rest it would heal slowly over the next few weeks. She had scratches and bruises on her body, but they were superficial. He gave her a prescription for Antibiotics and a month's supply of painkillers.

It was now 8pm, they had just finished a light supper and Laura looked through the kitchen window; there were so many trees in the back garden plus a large pool. 'She really was lucky last night and was thankful she hadn't fallen into that freezing water' Ray persuaded her to stay for the night, he had two spare bedrooms and neither had ever been used. Her suitcase was in one of them and he had washed and dried her clothes. However, he drew the line at ironing! When Laura was ready, she descended the stairs to the living room, and instead of the oversized shirt and Rays pyjama bottoms she worn all day. She wore a white fitted tight knit jumper, a knee length grey pencil skirt and black velvet low-heeled shoes. Her clothes fitted her figure perfectly. Ray's eyes stayed fixed on her as he sat in his armchair. Her hair hung loosely down her back, she looked at him and smiled. Her makeup was minimal, accentuating her natural features, which only made her even more desirable to him. He had never seen anyone more beautiful.

She settled on the sofa and told him more about her life. He felt happy knowing she trusted him enough to confide in him. For his part, he wanted to know everything he could about this stunning lady who was making such an impact on him. She told him about her time in care; she was five years old when she was taken and knew nothing of her life before then.

Children would come and go, but some stayed for years just like she did. At the age of 16 it was her time to leave the home. She made her way to the nearest city, and immediately found the waitress job at the nightclub then Laura fell silent and sadness filled her eyes. Ray noticed her expression, stood up and went over to her.

"Are you okay?" he asked, kneeling in front of her. She lifted her head; her eyes met his concerned stare.

"Yes, I'm fine," she reassured, "It's just that it saddens me to think that something that once felt so right could become so toxic." Then he said,

"I have never been in a long-term relationship, but I strongly believe that if something is right and good it will last forever and sadly the opposite is true too: if it is wrong and bad then it will stay that way?" His words made perfect sense to her, it was such a simple analysis of a confusing and damaging situation. Then she said. "I've never looked at it that way before. For years I felt that I was the one who had to change to help him cope better. It was like I was stripping layers of who I was away and slowly disappearing. The way I talked to people, the way I dressed or acted around them, but no matter what I did, it didn't stop him from being who he was? Then she went quiet. "How he behaved wasn't your fault because the problem was his, not yours. For years you tried everything to help him, but that man needs some serious professional help" he said. "Yes, I know," she whispered softly. "you are lucky you got away from him in one piece" he said. She knew that was also true. Despite the hurt she felt, she smiled. Then he asked her if she would like a drink. "Thank you, a hot chocolate would be lovely," she said. He decided on a glass of red wine. Laura felt relaxed after telling him more about herself, she looked at the clock, it was 9 pm.

They talked for another hour and then decided to call it a night. Laura hadn't slept in a bed since leaving the city. The clean sheets and warm blanket felt heavenly and as soon as her head hit the pillow, she fell asleep. Ray lay awake, thinking about what Laura had told him, he couldn't believe what she had been through, but now she was here, and he would help her become stronger, in any way he could.

Destiny Rose

CHAPTER SIX --- THE JOURNEY

Martin had been driving non-stop for almost two hours; hitting high speeds, going well over 100mph when he knew there were no speed cameras. Deminick was a long way behind them and the radio was playing. Bret had been unusually quiet, and Martin broke the silence, "Do you remember when we first came to this city, Bret?" Martin asked. "Yeah, such a long time ago" Bret replied. "It sure was, and we haven't done so badly, have we?"

"No, we've done okay, and if I can just get Laura to come back with me, then everything will be perfect again."

"Bret, what if Laura doesn't want to come back. Have you thought about that?" Bret looked at Martin, "she has to come back, she knows how much I need her. I know I haven't been the best husband, but I need her, and she needs me, she understands me." Desperation was evident in his voice.

Martin was worried about him; he was convinced that, when they did eventually catch up with her, she'd refuse to come back. He had to try and make Bret see sense for his own sake. He couldn't stay silent.

"Bret, you know I wouldn't say anything to upset you, but you need to listen to what I'm saying. You may have to give up on her if she doesn't want to come back. There's not a lot we can do about it. There are some things we have to accept in life and move on," he said. Bret looked at him, "I am listening Martin, but I don't agree, I'm not giving up on her, no way. She is just angry, we were meant to be together and as for accepting things, well we both know that accepting things doesn't take the pain away. So why would I want to live in even more pain than I already was, without her. She will forgive me; I know she will?" Martin's head was working overtime. Somehow, he had to get

Destiny Rose

through to Bret that if Laura didn't want to come back, he would have to leave her behind, but, for now, Martin would leave the subject alone.

As soon as they arrived at the station, they immediately noticed there wasn't any surveillance cameras installed, which was a disappointment. The shop doubled as a café, and a young lady behind the counter greeted them. Bret didn't hesitate and took a picture of Laura out of his pocket. He told her Laura was his sister and hadn't been heard of after travelling this way while going for a job interview a week ago. The woman studied the picture; she wanted to help this handsome man find his sister, but she hadn't seen her, then she shouted out for the café owner who was in the back kitchen. Her boss Louie joined them; he was a small, jolly man. Completely Bald but with a thick black moustache curled into handlebars at the ends! "Welcome, welcome, gentlemen, whatever can we do for you?" Martin told him the same story Bret had given. Louie took the picture and immediately recognized Laura.

"Delightful, bountiful, beautiful" he shouted out as though he was declaring it to the world! "How could someone forget such a beauty, so dark, so perfect, and …." but before he could add another word, Bret snatched the picture out of his hand and snapped. "Okay, we get it but, she's my sister so less of the lingo pal." Then Martin said, "We need to find her in case she is in some sort of trouble, so any information at all, would be helpful?" Louie told them she paid by cash, and what direction she'd drove off in, and that was all he could remember. Martin slipped the man a couple of twenty-pound notes and told him to treat himself to a bottle of fine wine. They stayed in the café, had something to eat and rested for a while. Neither of them felt positive; it could possibly take weeks to find her at this rate, then.

Destiny Rose

"We might have better luck further down the line" Bret said. Martin agreed, she would have stayed somewhere to sleep overnight, there will be other places that remember her. They filled up the car and Louie came dashing out of the shop, his arms waving "Gentlemen I remember something else. Her car had a big black letter V on the front grille and one on the boot." Then he bid them a good day.

They already knew the colour of the car, from the sighting by the HGV driver, but they hadn't known the model. "well that narrows it down a bit, now we have something more solid." Martin said. "It more than narrows it down a bit, it makes us closer to finding her quicker than I thought" Bret took over at the wheel, and Martin decided to call a friend who also happened to be a police inspector.

Tony Ratchet was sat at his desk when he answered Martins call. He told him they were worried about Laura and gave him details about the car she was travelling in. Tony wrote all the information down and said he would be in touch if he could find out anything. After a brief chat about business the conversation ended.

Over the next two days they stopped at all cafés, shops and any places they thought she may have visited. There had been a few sightings and were confident they were travelling in the right direction. They had slept overnight in motels on route and had heard nothing from Tony Ratchet.

Today was Friday, it was 3pm and Bret had been driving for over an hour, "I could do with something to drink, my throat's gone dry," he said. They saw a sign for a newsagent shop and followed the directions. Inside the shop Martin grabbed a newspaper and asked the shopkeeper, an elderly man, if he had seen Laura. The man looked at the picture and remembered her, he knew the day and exact time, because he was pulling the shutters down and she raced down the road, desperate to know where the next petrol station was, which was Little Hampton. He told them he had been worried about her because she was in such a rush and look tired. Then the man said, "Maybe I should have rung the police, my information could have helped you find her sooner, I do hope she is found safe and well?" The men could see he was deeply concerned, and Martin said. "You've done nothing wrong and she's not officially missing and has done this before. She was staying with friends and didn't bother telling anyone. I think we just worry too much, you know what brothers are like?" Then Bret thanked him for the information, got back in the car and drove off. They continued driving for another hour and came across a Premier Inn sign. They both needed a rest from the road so followed the sign into a small, quaint, picturesque village.

They found the Hotel and enjoyed a hearty meal but neither had any alcohol, choosing to stay teetotal on this journey. They were relaxing in the lounge and Martin decided he would try to talk to Bret again,

"Bret, have you thought that maybe Laura just wants to make a fresh start somewhere else? She wouldn't have left unless she was serious and had planned it," he said, Bret stared at him, "A fresh start? You make it sound so easy Martin: she can't possibly forget everything we had, and just leave 'at the drop of a hat, that would be insane?" he replied. "Insane to us but not to her, like I said, she could have planned this for months, perhaps it wasn't just on a whim or done in an angry moment." Bret thought about Martin's words, then said. "Are people's feelings that disposable to someone who's supposed to love you. Why can't she forgive me? Martin listened to Bret's every word, he had to get through to him somehow. "Bret, people's feelings change, that doesn't mean you are less that man she first met. Nothing is ever just black or white. Some things can become complex, your anger sometimes gets the better of you and you know you will never change, over time slowly it's got worse when it comes to Laura. Maybe she just got tired, splitting up might be just what both of you need, we can concentrate on business then, just me and you, as it was all them years ago? Martin saw the sadness in Bret's eyes. "I know it was a lot for her to put up with, but I love her. I've never loved anyone the way I love her, and she loved me. I know she will come back to me if I could just explain things to her? then he went silent. Martin looked at him, "It's okay, somehow, we will sort this mess out?

(Martin didn't know exactly how he was going to do that but, he knew he had to try.)

It was 6.30pm when they left the Hotel. Their next stop would be the petrol station in Little Hampton.

Destiny Rose

CHAPTER SEVEN --- LITTLE HAMPTON

The week passed quickly in Little Hampton and today was Friday. Ray had convinced Laura to stay with him until her course of Antibiotics had finished, and her rib healed. They visited Marcy's cottage on the Sunday and the ladies immediately took to each other. Ray had lied to her about Laura's arrival in the village, something which neither he nor Laura liked doing. However, he felt it was for the best, he didn't want Marcy to worry needlessly, and she would if she knew the true story. He told Marcy, Laura was the daughter of his father's friend and was in the area on business.

Laura had taken a shine to Charlie and during the week visited the cottage and taken the dog out for walks in the woods. Gossip about the car crash had been the hot topic in the village, so they avoided going there.

Ray took her to work during the latter part of the week showing her around the complex. His office was messy, and Laura enjoyed tidying it up. "It's an organized mess" he had told her, and Laura had laughed.

'At work these days Ray mostly signed on dotted lines that his secretary would have left on his desk. As a policeman he had investigated hundreds of burglaries and saw the upset it caused. He knew there was a need to provide more high-quality security alarm systems for homes and businesses. He had over 100 people working for him, plus a small team of inventors with new ideas. The latest was fingerprint identification, which could be used to open doors, so people wouldn't have any use for a key, you could even switch your lights, TV or music system on without having to flick a switch and your print had to be paired with a system or device for your use.'

Ray had enjoyed taking Laura into work - it had made a welcome change to his usual routine and now the week was over, and they were on their way home, he pulled up at Robert and Frances Stirling's petrol station. He filled his tank and as soon as he walked into the shop to pay, he heard. "Hello there, Mr. Maitland," a jolly and deep Scottish voice bellowed out.

"Hello, Robert, hope you're well?"

"Yes, thank you, Frances has just nipped to the bakery; and should be back any minute now, but you know what women are like, she's probably having a good natter. I hope she'll be back before closing time" he said, Ray laughed and handed over his payment. "Have you ever tried Mrs. Miller's homemade cottage pie, Mr. Maitland?" Robert asked. "No, I haven't," Ray replied.

"It's a real treat, she makes the best pie for miles, but don't tell my Frances I said that, or she'll have me on bread and water for a month." Ray Laughed, "I won't tell her, and we all deserve a treat every now and again." Then he glanced through the window to check Laura was okay. Robert noticed her in the car. "Oh, I'm sorry, I didn't realise you had a lady friend waiting, you are usually alone?"

"No problem Robert; it's a pleasure as always. Give my regards to Frances." The men bid each other good evening. Then Ray walked back to the car. Laura giggled as soon as he sat down and said, "men, you are worse than women for chatting." Ray laughed.

It was a pleasant evening. Ray decided to take Laura to the high cliff in Little Hampton, he parked the car in a lay-by near the cliff

Destiny Rose

and taking her hand walked her to the edge of the hill, she was amazed she didn't know there was a sea so close to them and the view was fantastic. She looked down and saw the shoreline. There was at least a twenty-foot drop; and she was in awe at the sight. A sandy beach strewn with rocks, rugged and natural. Then Ray told her it was only a fifteen-minute walk through the woods, to his house. "Good Lord, if I'd gone a different way last week, I could have walked off this cliff that night and ended up in the sea?" She said.

"Well thank God you didn't and instead of finding the sea, you found me" he joked. He then explained there was no direct access to the beach and that it wasn't safe going down there, because, they were only small coves in this area, and could become dangerous places very quickly. However, the fishermen had made one or two pathways down to some of the coves, so anyone who knew the times of the tides could go down.

"Look, there's a pathway over there," he said, gesturing to a handmade wooden sign with an arrow pointing downwards. "I have never been to a cove before. Can we go down and have a look?" she asked excited by the idea...

"Luckily the tide is out we have about an hour before it comes in, so yes, we can" he replied.

Still holding her hand lay Red her down a narrow, gravel, sloping path. Wild-flowers and thick clumps of grass were all around their feet. The cove was a stunning little place a real hidden gem. It was a rough circular space, about 50 feet in diameter and the sand looked golden from down here. It was cleaner than she had envisioned. There was a small cave opening in the cliff wall. He walked her to the water's edge.

"It's beautiful, thank you for showing it to me." she said. They stood looking out at the waves thrashing around in the sea. Then he led her back and to the entrance to the cave in the cliff's wall. He told her how the cave, just like many others scattered around

were once used by smuggler's, who would hide all sorts of illegal cargo in them. "It's a magical and special place," she said.
Ray looked at her "it is a special place for a special lady" he replied. Laura smiled. "A place is one of the world's natural beauties, just like you." He added and Laura blushed. He was right about it being natural and beautiful, but she felt embarrassed by his compliment and joked. "I think for objects that are closest to you, you may need glasses Mr. Maitland." Ray laughed. His laugh echoed around the cove. "I'm being completely honest" he said. She smiled, and still holding her hand they made their way back up to the top of the cliff. Ray said he would take her back to the cove again, maybe in the summertime when it was warm enough to bring along a picnic. The idea filled Laura with happiness, then suddenly reality dawned on her.

"But I may be far away by then?" she said and came to a halt. Ray stopped walking too and looked at her.

"Do you want to be somewhere else Laura, away from here, away from me??" She stayed quiet, she was stunned by his words; it wasn't so much what he said, but the way she felt when he said them. The thought of not seeing him or Marcy and the dog again, made her feel sick. She couldn't imagine saying goodbye. Ray saw the confusion on her face, "I don't want you to leave Laura," he said, "I don't want to leave either. I don't feel ready to leave any of this behind, "she replied, her eyes still focused on his. "Well, you don't have to go, nothing is forcing you. We can see how you feel after a few weeks" he said, a smile took over his face, Laura smiled too. Ray was hooked on Laura; she had walked into his life and now he wanted her to stay in it. He would take one day at a time and enjoy each one.

Laura had left her husband just over a week ago, and decided to stay well away from men for a long time, but she was falling for this man… She wasn't confused about her feelings for him,

Destiny Rose

he was caring, kind and intelligent, all she had ever wanted in a man. She had felt alone for many years, and now something magical was happening to her. In silence they made their way back to the car.

Marcy closed her sitting room curtains, picked up the book she was currently reading and sat down in her rocking chair by the open fire. Laura had surprised Marcy a few times during the week by dropping in on her, usually just before 6pm. They would have a chat and a cup of tea, and she would take Charlie for a short walk, but it was now 7pm and felt sure Laura wouldn't be calling by tonight.

It was 7.30pm when Ray and Laura got home, I will ring Marcy, she will be settled in for the night by now, so I will go tomorrow." Laura said, hanging her coat up. Ray nodded and headed to the kitchen to make them both a warm drink.

"I've really enjoyed this past week." Ray said as he brought their drinks in. Laura was sat on the sofa and he sat down in his chair. and he continued.

"I should be thanking you because all my office notes and files are in order now." Laura giggled. Ray watched her face light up, he liked to see her laugh and smile. "You have a beautiful smile," he said. Laura's face reddened by his compliment; she took a sip of her hot chocolate. Realising his brashness, he said

"I'm sorry. I didn't mean to embarrass you."

"You haven't, it was a lovely compliment, thank you." he replied and at this moment their eyes locked onto each other and they both smiled. Then she joked "and your cups of hot chocolate are simply the best."

"I'm glad you like them, and I am glad you are here with me" he replied, holding his gaze on her. She took another sip of her chocolate and Ray asked if he could join her on the sofa, she nodded. He sat down beside her. She cupped her mug and drank slowly, while she thought about her feelings for the man beside her.

"You can put your drink down it isn't going to grow legs and run off," he joked. Laura laughed, and for a moment forgot she was still holding the mug in her hands and the chocolate splashed out a little. Ray put his hands over the cup steadying it, they looked at each other and then burst into laughter, he took her mug and placed it on the coffee table, then he moved a little closer to her and quietly said, "Laura, do you remember last week when I said to you that maybe the angels had sent you to me?"

"Yes, I remember. "she replied, "well, I want you to know after the week with you I still think the angels sent you to me." Laura's eyes filled with the softest of tears, overwhelmed by the tenderness emanating from such a strong man. He continued.

"When you first opened your eyes that night on my sofa my heart skipped a beat, and I have felt the same ever since."

Laura was drowning in his words, her eyes filling with tears at the thought of being blessed to have met such a caring and charming man. She moved closer to him and looking him in the eye she said, "maybe the angels brought you to me," and she gave him the sweetest smile he'd ever seen. His arm went around her waist and he pulled her closer to him. Her heartbeat faster, then he kissed her gently. Laura met him with the same tenderness, he stroked her long dark silken hair, and she felt his powerful chest beating against her own. Waves of utter pleasure washed through her. Then he swept her up into his arms and carried her up the stairs and into the bedroom.

They spent that night making true and magical love until the early hours, then Laura fell asleep in his arms.

Destiny Rose

CHAPTER EIGHT --- ANSWERS

It was 6.45pm when Martin pulled into the petrol station in Little Hampton. It was a small station with only two pumps and no CCTV. Mrs. Stirling greeted Bret as he entered the shop and immediately, he showed her Laura's photo. Frances picked up her spectacles and studied the picture carefully but was certain she'd never seen the lady before.

"Sorry no, I haven't but you could wait for my husband to return if you like. We shut at 7.30pm so he should be back soon, he has nipped into the village to see if Mrs. Miller has any pies left, and why he would want one of her pies is beyond me, when I can make them better than anyone around here!" She said.

Bret stood silent, he really wasn't in the mood for chatting about nonsense, nevertheless he forced a smile. Martin distracted him by walking into the shop and said. "I have enough for this fill but then I'm out nearly out of cash. How much do you have on you Bret?" Bret had less than Martin and asked the old lady if there was a cash machine nearby. She informed him there was one in the village on the post office wall and joked that if they saw her husband on the way to tell him to get back quickly or she'd lock up early and leave him. They paid her for the petrol and then headed off to find the village. It wasn't long before the two men arrived in Little Hampton.

The village was easy to find, it was a small place consisting of only four main streets. Most of the shops were closed, they parked up and walked to the cash machine. Martins mobile rang and Tony Ratchet informed him a car matching the same colour and model as the one they were looking for had been found abandoned at the side of a road, he gave the location and Martin

Destiny Rose

couldn't believe their luck. "We are in Little Hampton right now" he said and looked at Bret. Tony told him the car wasn't registered in anybody's name, and the last place the car was documented, was 6 months ago in a used car market. They investigated the area for two days and found nothing, no hospital reports, nothing came up. Martin looked at Bret. "This sounds promising Tony, we will let you know tomorrow how we get on" Martin said, then their call ended. Martin told Bret what Tony said that the car was in a local compound. Bret couldn't believe their luck too, and he said,

"finding her might be quicker than they thought this morning. Martin said. Bret agreed then said. "This is Fate: Fate brought us together and now it's reuniting us. "Maybe, but let's not get our hopes up, if that car was hers, she could have caught a train or a bus to somewhere else by now." "Yeah, let's see what tomorrow brings and take it from there" Bret replied. Martin nodded, "At least we know we are heading in the right direction" Bret agreed, he felt more optimistic now, that they would catch up with her.

It was 7.25pm, and they needed to find a room for the night, as they walked up and down the main street, they noticed rooms to let above a tea shop. Martin drove the car around and parked conveniently outside the shop, a sign located next to a winding set of metal stairs pointed the way to the entrance. Martin loudly knocked at the door, which was answered by a kindly looking elderly lady, she led them into the living room where her husband was sprawled out on a worn looking armchair. The room was adorned with green, leaf patterned curtains, floral settee and a heavy flower-patterned carpet; it looked like a botanist's nightmare from the 1970s. The lady introduced herself as Nancy and her husband, Henry, but told them to call them Mr. and Mrs. Cavanna if they preferred. Martin explained they worked for a public telephone company and were doing a survey in rural villages. The couple were delighted at the idea: they'd spent all their lives here and they loved the old buildings and the cobbled streets, but it did lack technology! "We only have one phone box for the whole village, and if that breaks, we have none" Nancy informed them. Martin told her they would note down her concern's tomorrow.

"You will be the very first person we talk to though Nancy." Bret said. Her face immediately lit up, she felt honoured!

"You must have come a long way, "she said. Noticing they were wearing smart suits and knowing the nearest city was 74 miles away. Martin confirmed her thoughts, and then explained they'd been travelling for days visiting places along the way.

"Poor things, you must be worn out, all that driving, are you hungry, do you want me to make you something to eat?" she said. The men were hungry, but Martin didn't want to put on the dear lady and replied. "No, we are both fine we ate just an hour ago." Then she said. "How about a nice cup of tea, a cup of tea won't hurt you?" and without waiting for an answer she bustled her way to the kitchen.

Bret went to get their luggage from the car and the pot of tea was on the marble coffee table when he returned! "No-one can make a pot of tea quicker than I" she said, and her husband nodded in agreement, Martin held his laughter in.
Bret Sat down and put the luggage at his feet. The teapot was as old-fashioned as the room, it had a very long spout and a matching set of cups and saucers. A thick knitted tea cosy covered the whole of its body.

"This is my best china, it is called the willow pattern; no one ever gets fed up with the willow pattern" she said, as she poured the men a cup of tea her husband nodded in agreement. A smile forced its way onto Bret's face, and Martin felt like he was going to burst out laughing, but he suppressed the urge.

"It's a fine-looking teapot," Martin said. Bret then explained they were expecting to meet up with a work colleague in the village, and he showed them a picture of Laura. They both looked at the image but neither of them had seen her. After their tea they were shown to their room on the top floor, then she gave Martin two sets of keys one for the room and the other for the main door to the house and asked them if they wanted breakfast in the morning. The men declined, Martin explained they never ate in the mornings, but always made up for it at dinnertime and she smiled.

Their room was surprisingly modern in contrast to the living room. It was basic with two single beds and good enough to sleep in. They unpacked a few things and it wasn't long before they were asleep.

Saturday morning. Ray woke up at 6am and watched Laura as she slept. Her head was resting on his chest and her hair fell onto his stomach, he kissed her cheek ever so softly. The feelings they shared last night were the best he'd ever felt, he had never wanted to show another woman as much love as he'd shown her last night.

He watched her sleep for a while, then eased his way out of bed and went downstairs.

At 10am Laura opened her eyes and there was an empty space beside her, it was 10 am. Her hand went to the spot where Ray had been sleeping and she rested it there for a moment. Her whole being was full of the passion she had felt last night. She had never experienced anything like this before, and her body was shouting out for him right now, she it wanted to feel more. She stroked the sheet where Ray had lay and then he poked his head around the bedroom door. "Good morning sleeping beauty," he joked. Laura's face lit up at the sight of him, and although fully dressed he lay down next to her.

Destiny Rose

"Good morning," she replied and gave a big smile. Ray playfully stroked the tip of her nose, which made Laura's smile even broader and within seconds he was kissing her, and they spent the morning once again lost in their desire.

Bret was showered and dressed by 6.00am. Martin was asleep, so he decided to go for an early morning walk. The shops were shut and the street empty, he walked past the shops, and spotted a large handmade wooden sign next to a clear opening into the woods. The sign was for fishing and he followed the arrow pointing to a pathway inside the trees, his thoughts went to Laura and he wondered what she was doing right now. What if she was lost out here somewhere in these trees or injured and not able to call for help? he couldn't understand why she would abandon her car. If she had stayed with it, the police would have helped her. Or maybe she found another way to travel and was safe and miles away from here. Thoughts looped around his head and he analysed each one, eventually he decided that there was no use in speculating. He couldn't answer the questions in his head, and to dwell on them would only wreck it.

It wasn't long before he came across a stream and an old man was sat on a wooden stool fishing. The man was surprised to see Bret; he'd fished this area for years and he had never seen such a smartly dressed young fellow around here. "Hi there, how's it going?" the old guy called out. Bret walked to his side and explained how he and his work colleague were here in the village on business. The man introduced himself as Ted Baker and started to talk about the trout in the stream, Bret had never cared much for fishing it bored him, but still he listened to the man. He was around sixty years of age, with a long grey beard, a green flat cap covered his long silver hair; he wore green wading boots, over dark brown canvas dungarees, and looked exactly what Bret expected a fisherman to look like!

Destiny Rose

"You're up early on a Saturday, isn't it a day of rest?" the man said, Bret nodded and replied, "You don't get to see much of the countryside when you live and work in the city, so I thought I'd explore the area to see what I could find."

"Do you know we have a sea here, but we don't have any don't public beaches, plenty of little coves down there though, we made our own signposts to pathways that lead you safely down, it's just a ten-minute walk, but don't go down to the coves unless you have all the information about when the tides come in. You don't want to get trapped down there" Ted said. Bret was keen to see the sea, so he got directions and headed off. A short while later he was standing on the clifftop next to the handmade signposts pointing the way down. In the exact spot Laura had stood last night.

He looked out across the sea, the view was stunning, he didn't want to walk down the pathway to the beach below. He took in the views then headed back to the village.

Martin slept till 10am, Bret told him about his walk. Them martin said he was going to have a shower, "I could really do with a drink of pure orange" he added. "I can nip to the newsagent's I will get a litre carton, is there anything else we need?"

"No, I can't think of anything - just the juice will do for now, thanks" Martin replied. As soon as Bret walked into the newsagent's a middle-aged couple behind the counter, and an elderly lady customer turned to look at him. "Good Morning" he said confidently, all three-stayed silent and looked him up and down and immediately he felt out of place… Then the woman behind the counter smiled and said.

"Good morning young man, what can we do for you on this fine day?" The customer, an old lady stepped away from the front of the counter and moved to the side, and with her hand she beckoned him to come closer.

"Come forward dear we don't bite, and if I tried you then don't fear because I have false teeth and if I chew on anything to hard, they fall out" she said and gave a smile. Bret forced a smile and walked to the counter; the shop was small with just enough room for the old lady and him standing side by side. The lady kept her eyes on Bret he could feel them boring into him. "Florence, give the man some room to breathe?" The man behind the counter bellowed out, then he turned to Bret and said, "take no heed of our Flo here, she is teasing you, she isn't used to seeing smart young men around here" the ladies giggled.

The lady behind the counter said. "I'm Patricia Dawson young man and take no heed of my husband Jim, he is just jealous because he's not the only good-looking one around here now, you are his competition" and Jim laughed. Bret told them he was in the village on business; the trio didn't keep him long and after a brief chat he left with his orange juice. He intended to head straight back to his room but the smell from the bakery wafted over to him, prompting him to get some croissants to take back to the room too. He walked into the shop and a customer was talking to the shopkeeper who was preparing an order. The door was wedged open and they didn't notice him walk in. Bret stood in silence, listening to the ladies talking.

"Marcy, if you ever need an extra custard, I can put one away for you, just ring me first thing in the morning next time," Mrs. Miller, the shopkeeper said. Marcy replied, "but I don't like to mess you around. I didn't realise until this morning that Laura would be calling tonight. She should have called yesterday, and an egg custard would be a lovely treat for her." Bret froze as he heard the name 'Laura!' Was this his Laura? Then Marcy continued.

"Charlie really missed her last night, but I'm sure I will find out today why she never came?" Bret focused on the name 'Charlie.'

Destiny Rose

"who the hell was Charlie? Anger filled him inside and he gave a little cough, interrupting the women.

"Hello, so sorry I didn't hear you come in, can I help you dear?" Mrs. Miller said looking at him. Bret was silently stunned for a moment, then Marcy smiled at him, we wanted to ask right now who this Laura was, but Martin's rational words came into his mind. 'Don't panic. Take in a deep breath and stay calm'. Bret had to be careful, because if it was his Laura, then why hadn't she rung him, to tell him that she was okay after crashing her car? Why would she be with these people? He introduced himself and then explained how he was here on business, and with the help of a college were compiling a survey. The ladies started to talk about the village and amenities it had. Eventually Mrs. Miller asked Bret what he would like from the shop, he was still deciding, he said, so she carried on with Marcy's order. Bret listened as they went back to their conversation. Marcy continued to tell Mrs. Miller how good it had been since Laura had come into their lives.

'Their lives'? The words rang around Bret's mind, he had to find out if this woman was talking about his Laura, he looked at the hot-cross buns on the top of the counter. and said that he would take a couple, Bret then talked to the women about how technology was fast advancing, and they listened with interest. After their chat, Marcy was ready to head home, Bret immediately asked her if he could help her with her bag and suggested that she could give him more insight about the lack of services in the area. Marcy beamed with pride that he wanted her advice and she passed her shopping bag to him. They bid Mrs. Miller good day and made their way to Marcy's cottage. It was only a fifteen-minute walk and Charlie were excited to see a new person walk into the house with Marcy.

"This is Charlie" she said, and he stroked the dog and noticed quickly that Marcy lived alone, she asked if he wanted a cup of

Destiny Rose

tea and a scone and he accepted, then she told him a little about herself and then asked if he had enjoyed his scone, adding. "I hope it wasn't doughy?" Bret looked at her, puzzled for a moment.

"No, it was fine, thank you." and then it happened... Everything he wanted to know came flooding out, as she told him how Laura had baked the scones only yesterday and that she was new to the village, then told him about her job as a housekeeper and how it was just a short walk through the pathway in the woods to Ray's house, and about Laura visiting her each evening without fail for a chat and to walk Charlie. Marcy talked for over an hour and Bret listened to every word, and then he bid her a good day, she waved him off with Charlie standing beside her his tail wagging.

'What a lovely, polite young man' she thought as she headed back into the living room, then sat down and picked up her book.

Bret had listened to the old lady for longer than he wanted, her words spun around his head as he made his way back to his room.

'Laura and Ray were just friends and that she wanted to her live around here forever.' Rage filled him, but he knew he had to stay calm, later that evening Marcy wouldn't be the only one waiting for Laura and the only place she would be living was in City, with him, and whoever this Ray was, he had better not get in his way or he would be one sorry son of a bitch.

Martin was dressed when Bret returned. "Did you go to Deminick for that juice?" he joked, but Bret was in no laughing mood and filled Martin in on everything that had just happened. Martin immediately thought about Kay, he could be home much quicker than he had expected after all… Bret didn't feel happy, he was just relieved that he had found her, but she was with another man, and he was angry.

"I'm fuming Martin, if she's with another guy, I will rip his head off" Bret said. "Bret, you just said they were just friends, and you thought a dog was a man? You need to stay calm, you really do" Martin replied.

"Just friends… how many times have we both heard that one?" he replied still angry. Then Martin calmly said, "We need to stay focused here, or you could mess this up, he could be 65 or even 80. Everyone around here seems old, I bet you haven't seen one young person yet?" Bret knew Martin was right; they discussed the best way to handle the meeting tonight. Bret wanted to get her to somewhere quiet, so they could talk over everything. Then the little cove came into his mind, the fisherman had told him about.

"The cove, it's a perfect place, we can all go there it's quiet too." Martin agreed.

Destiny Rose

CHAPTER NINE --- FACE TO FACE

It was 4.45pm and Martin and Bret were approaching Marcy's cottage. They had talked about how they would approach Laura when they saw her, Martin wasn't keen on the idea of surprising her in the middle of some forest but he wanted this to be over sooner rather than later and by night-time it would be. Bret pointed to the path in the trees at the side of the cottage and they walked into the wood, the further they went the darker it got as the trees closed in on them. The light grey gravel path stood out well and after a few minutes they found the perfect spot to hide.

They took cover behind some trees and patiently waited. It was over an hour wait when they saw he view and as soon as she was near enough Bret rushed out and grabbed her from behind.

Laura screamed but quickly he covered her mouth with his hand and held her tight. Martin stood in front of her, he saw fear in her eyes, and he felt ashamed by his actions. She kicked her legs out at him, but he took hold of her ankles holding them firm, they wasted no time at all and carried her off deep into the trees. Laura was kicking frantically but Martin kept his grip, and when they were well away from the cottage he said.

"Bret, you'll have to take your hand from her mouth soon and give her some air, she's struggling to breathe?"

"She'll be fine Martin, she can breathe through her nose, you heard her screaming back there. If I take my hand away, she'll start again." Bret seemed to have no compassion at all for Laura and Martin was starting to feel worried about the situation. Tears were falling, she was terrified. Martin told her that Bret only wanted to talk to her somewhere quiet and afterwards they could all go back to their lives. He promised her that everything would be okay. Laura was in shock, but Martin's words gave her a little comfort.

'Martin had always been respectful to her from the first day she met him. They both knew how irrational Bret could be, but she had to put her faith in him and trust what he said.'

Inside the cottage, Charlie heard Laura's scream, the echo reached its way to him. Immediately he went to the front door and whimpered. Marcy was in the kitchen; the kettle was on Charlie walked into the kitchen making a low groaning noise, and then returned to the front door whimpering again. 'Whatever has gotten into that dog?' she had never seen him so agitated and raising her voice she said. "She will take you for a walk when she gets here you will just have to wait"

Five minutes passed; Marcy placed the tea tray down on the coffee table in the middle of the room. The tea-cosy would keep the pot nice and warm. She looked to the clock: it was 5.15pm.

The men reached the clifftop, they were still holding her. Bret explained they were all going down to the cove below. Staying calm, she nodded but inside she was terrified. His hand was still over her mouth and she couldn't speak. Martin let go of her legs then Bret said if she promised not to scream, he would remove his hand, she nodded again, and he took his hand away but kept a firm grip on her arm.

Laura was scared to scream in case Bret lashed out at her and knocked her over the edge of the cliff, so she remained silent. She looked at Martin; he saw that she was putting all her faith in him, to help her, Martin gave a forced smile. Bret guided her towards the pathway to the cove and Laura pleaded with him

Destiny Rose

"Bret, please , we can talk up here, the sea could come in quickly and at any time," Bret took no notice and carried on, Martin walked behind them, reassuring her not to be scared, and that everything would be all right. Deep down Laura knew this talk with Bret had to be done, because she wanted to be left alone, she didn't want Bret finding out about Ray and possibly hurting him, she just wanted Bret to leave her alone, so she could try and make another life for herself.'

Charlie refused to move from the front door, and he started to bark. Marcy looked at the clock it was 5. 30pm. Maybe she should take him a walk-in case he needed to do something, so she decided to ring Ray and let him know she would take the dog for a little walk before Laura got here. Ray was surprised to hear Marcy voice on the phone and Charlie was still barking. He was shocked when Marcy told him Laura had not arrived yet, panic filled him. "She left over an hour ago, wanting to be early because she never saw you yesterday, she should have been with you ages ago?"

"Maybe, she met one of the locals on the path, she could be still out there chatting to them" Marcy said. Then Charlie started to scratch at the front door, she had never seen him act like this before. He was really rattled by something. "The dog is acting strange Ray really unsettled?" she said. Ray felt unsettled too. "I am coming to yours, don't open the front door because there could be a fox or even two out there, I will be with you in five minutes."

Marcy looked through the peephole on her door, but saw nothing, no foxes, no cats, even so she would do as Ray asked, and not open the door until he arrived. Ray walked with a fast pace on the same route Laura used but there wasn't sight or sound of her, and he felt worried. She opened the door to his knock and Charlie tried to get outside, but Ray caught hold of his collar. The dog was struggling to break free. Fear quickly filled Ray, he had never seen him act like this before, even if he spotted a fox on one of his walks, he was never this wild over it something was wrong, he could feel it. He kept holding the dog's collar and looked at Marcy she was worried too.

"It will be a couple of foxes running around, don't worry Marcy, I will take him out for a good walk we will probably bump into Laura out there" She handed him Charlies lead,

"Okay dear, be careful out there" she said. Ray put the lead on the dog's collar. He opened the door and like a runaway train Charlie darted off, he broke free from Rays hold and ran into the woods. Ray raced after him.

Panic filled Marcy, Charlie was frantic to get outside, and Ray looked worried sick. Something was wrong, she. picked up the phone and rang the police station.

Bret, Martin, and Laura stood facing each other in the cove. Bret tried hard to convince Laura to go home with him, but she was determined, she didn't want to go.

"Bret, let me have some peace and a chance of trying to create a new life," she pleaded. However, Bret was furious that she wanted to carry on without him, he tried again to get her to change her mind, promising her he would change if she came back, but she didn't change her mind, and she said, "I haven't had the best of starts in this life as you know, and I just want to move on and find some peace and normality, can't you allow me to have a little bit of that?" and he looked at him sincerely, but there was no compassion in Bret's eyes at all. There was nothing but anger, and tears slowly rolled down her cheeks.

"Please, Bret, please, I've had enough," she repeated. Bret looked at her, he knew he'd lost her. She was afraid of him; she would never look at him in the same way as she had when they first met. All he could see in her face was fear and the need to be as far away from him as possible. Rage filled him, and he shouted.

"You want to live in peace with another man, you mean. I could smell him on you as I carried you. I bet you met him at my nightclub, didn't you? I bet you both planned this whole thing, didn't you?" he stared furiously at her. Martin took hold of Bret's arm. "she isn't with another man, that's not true mate, she just wants to make a fresh start?" Bret pulled away from his grip and looked at him. "A fresh start, so it's that simple is it, how do we know she isn't with another man, do we really know anything about this bitch, we don't really know what she is capable of" Martin was puzzled. "What are you talking about Bret, of course we do? "She is no better than that scumbag in the children's home. Abuse and use you and then spit you out, with no thought for the damage they do."

Laura's head was spinning, she couldn't believe that yesterday she was stood in this spot and felt nothing but love, and now all she heard was hate and felt fear. She was sure she was going to faint, but she had to hold it together. She desperately wanted to calm Bret down and shouted out, "No Bret, I swear to you that this wasn't planned. I didn't know anybody when I came here" Then Martin shouted. "Bret, what the hell is wrong with you, she is nothing like Surringer. You are the one terrifying her not the other way around, and it's about time you stopped, just let her go its over" he demanded. Bret turned to Martin and looking him straight in the eye shouted. "So, you are saying that I am like that monster, me doing this to her, is like what that monster did to me, too, you are fucking insane Martin?" Bret put his hand inside his jacket pocket and pulled out the gun, and he pointed it at Martin.

Martin couldn't believe what he was seeing. Bret kept his eyes on Martin but then turned the gun on Laura and full of rage shouted out "YOU WANT PEACE? I'LL GIVE YOU AS MUCH PEACE AS YOU WANT YOU BITCH" and he pulled the trigger. The bullet hit her directly in the chest and she slumped to the floor, within seconds the sand around her turned red. Martin fell to his knees "My God Bret what have you done; she needs am ambulance" he screamed out. He reached into his pocket for his mobile phone, then Bret pointed the gun at him.

"Don't you dare call for help Martin, or I will shoot you in the head" he said. Martin looked at him. Bret continued "you bring God into this Martin, a load of religious nonsense drummed into us by filthy lying bastards as soon as we could talk, it means nothing. A true God would ever have allowed what happened to me back then. You stopped him from hurting me Martin, not God, just you" and tears fell from his eyes. Martin pleased with him "Bret we make our own choices in this life, and we need to make the right ones; we cannot let the bastards who hurt us win. A bad, twisted evil person hurt you Bret, they do the Devils, dirty, soul destroying, deeds. Laura isn't bad or evil she shouldn't suffer because of who they are, and neither should you." Martin pointed at Laura and shouted, "She is as innocent, as you are Bret, we need to get her an ambulance." Bret looked deeply into Martin's eyes. "You just don't get it do you Martin, you can't help me anymore. She was the only one that could help me. I can't keep fighting to keep my dreams peaceful. I can't do it anymore, she took away any normality I possessed, just like that monster did. They have done this to me." Suddenly they both heard a barking dog. Bret turned the gun on himself and pointing it against the side of his head pulled the trigger. A big dog had come out of nowhere and jumped up at Bret, then Martin screamed out

Destiny Rose

"NOOOOOOOOO" he fell to his knees, tears were streaming down his face, he punched the ground with his fists. "NOOOO" he continued to shout...

The dog was now the dog beside Laura, then he heard a man shouting. Within seconds Ray entered the cove, immediately he saw Laura's lifeless body and terror ripped right through him. He rushed to her side, she was covered in blood., her pulse was weak, he wrapped his coat around her, and put his hand firm against the wound in her chest trying to stop blood from pouring out. He used his mobile to call the emergency services, then lifted her up in his arms, he carried her up to the top of the cliff as fast as he could, his mind in utter turmoil. 'This couldn't be happening, he couldn't lose her, not now, not ever' his mind screamed out.

Martin picked up the gun and full of rage threw it hard against the stone wall. He cursed the little piece of metal as though that alone had caused all this damage. He was angry with himself for not knowing that Bret owned a gun. Guns was something neither of them had ever got involved with, and he would never have thought that Bret would ever use one. His tears wouldn't stop, then gently he lifted Bret's body up and holding him close made his way up the path.

Sergeant Johnson heard Ray's call for help and was waiting for him at the top of the cliff. "An Ambulance is on its way" he shouted as he made his way to Ray who had fell to his knees, still holding her tight in his arms. Tears fell from Rays eyes and he began to rock her limp body in his arms. The Sergeant had seen many a man as broken as Ray was right now and all he could to help Ray, was to pat him on the shoulder. "Hang on in there, help will be here soon" he said.

Martin reached the top of the cliff with Bret in his arms, then he dropped to the floor and put his friend facing up on the ground. The Sergeant walked over to Martin who was covered in Bret's blood. "He shot himself in the head he is Dead" Martin shouted out. The Sergeant looked at Bret, for someone who had supposedly blew his brains out, the top of his head still looked to be intact, and he checked his pulse. " He isn't dead, he still has a pulse" the sergeant said... Martin stood up, " he can't be, I saw what he did, I saw the dog jump up at him at the same time but he still shot himself in the head" he shouted out. "Maybe the dog knocked his aim off at the last minute, I don't know, but, that man has a pulse, and he is very much alive" the Sergeant said.

The ambulance arrived within minutes and immediately took Laura from Ray. Martin carried Bret to the ambulance, "he is alive" he shouted out. Ray lunged towards him shouting,
"WHAT THE HELL DO YOU THINK YOU ARE DOING, THAT LUNATIC IS NOT TRAVELLING WITH HER" The Sergeant grabbed hold of Rays arms holding him tight. Martin stopped walking, "he has a pulse, he needs help" he said. Ray tried to break away from the Sergeants grip, but he couldn't. The ambulance crew took Bret from Martin and managed to fit in him on the ambulance floor and with siren on and lights flashing, they sped off. Martin looked at the Sergeant who was still holding Ray and said "I tried to stop him" Ray was furious, "YOU TRIED TO STOP HIM, WELL YOU DIDN'T DO A GOOD JOB OF THAT DID YOU?" and desperately tried to break free from the Sergeants hold, he wanted to put his hands around this strangers neck, but the sergeants grip got stronger, he looked at Martin and said,

"Whoever you are just stay silent, get into my car and lock the doors. You are coming to the station with me" Martin did as he asked.

The Seargent addressed Ray "I am not letting go of you and if you force my hand, I will have to arrest you for obstruction and neither of us wants that. I am calling another car, they will take you to the hospital as quick as possible, okay?" Ray nodded.

The second police car arrived with minutes. Charlie had stayed by Rays side until he was told to go home and obediently, he went. Ray went to the hospital and the Sergeant took Martin back to the station.

CHAPTER TEN --- MIRACLES CAN HAPPEN

Ray rushed into the accident and emergency department frantically asking questions about Laura. A nurse guided him to a small private room by the reception desk and shut the door behind them. She asked Ray who he was and then asked about Laura's next of kin. His heart sank heavily to the floor,

"Why, what's wrong, why do you want to know that?" She could see he was in shock. Then she explained, they were not allowed to discuss patients with anyone, unless they were family or next of kin. He explained that Laura had no family or next of kin and the man who'd shot her was her husband. He informed her that he'd be the one taking care of her from now on and she was living with him in Little Hampton. Then he looked down at his clothes; he was covered in her blood.

"I don't know what I'll do if I lose her" he desperately said. The nurse told him her name was Jenny and she had just started her shift so would be with him for the next few hours, then she took him to a comfortable family waiting room. "The doctor will come and update us as soon as its possible" she said, then went off to get him a warm drink and some porters clothes to change into. They sat together for over an hour, then a doctor entered the room.

"Hello, Mr. Maitland, I am Doctor Glover, Ray shook his hand. I am looking after Laura" he said, and told him that the bullet had luckily missed her heart, which would have been fatal, he then explained how the bullet had exploded in her left lung, damaging the whole of the lung and then he went quiet.

Destiny Rose

Ray looked at him and before he could open his mouth, the doctor continued, "she is in the best place and luck must be on her side because we have one the country's finest surgeons here, shadowing our own for a few weeks so she is in the safe hands, he will perform the surgery" Ray's mind was in turmoil, "Surgery what kind of surgery?" he shouted desperately.

Jenny sat beside Ray and gently put her hand on top of his. Ray went quiet and the doctor said, "She needs a lung transplant, Mr. Maitland"

Ray couldn't believe what he was hearing, just a few hours ago she was smiling, they were happy and now this… He held his head low and his mind went into deep thought, 'she is alive, that was the main thing, he told him-self and slowly pulled his thoughts together. He looked at the doctor "Please, please help her." He said. "We will do everything we can Mr. Maitland, stay strong for her. It will be a long night, but the nurse will keep you updated, you are welcome to stay overnight here in the family room as long as is needed" then he left the room.

Ray bowed his head down low; his mind was spinning. He should never have let her walk through those woods alone, then his thoughts went to Marcy, she would be worried sick by now. He pulled himself together and decided to phone her.

It was 8pm when Marcy answered the call, she told him a couple of friends sat in with her until Charlie returned, and a police woman arrived who the Sergeant had sent and told her Laura had been taken to hospital, but didn't have any more details. Ray needed to stay strong, he didn't want her to hear that he was afraid and falling apart. He didn't mention the shooting and told her that Laura had fallen over, banged her head and twisted her ankle, and may be in here for a few days, but was fine" he said, trying to reassure her. He told her that if it wasn't for Charlie, he wouldn't have found her so quick. Marcy was happy to hear that, and said

"He is such a good dog; he is sleeping now in front of the fire." Ray told her he would be staying in the hospital overnight and that he would ring her again in the morning. "Make sure you have something to eat Ray" she said, and their phone call ended. The nurse appeared and walked towards him, "I was just coming to check up on you" and she walked him to a drinks machine. Then they went back to the family room, she sat down next to him and said. "I know all about transplant surgery and the surgeons are amazing."

"I feel useless, I want to be with her, helping them help her?" he replied.

"She won't know you are there, they have put her in a deep sleep, so her body doesn't panic and inside is calm. Just being here for her will mean everything to her, and she will tell you that when she is better." Tears filled his eyes, she continued easing his worries and fears, and gradually he calmed down.

Jenny looked no more than 30 years of age, her dark hair was tied into a neat bun on top of her head, her kind eyes, quiet voice and wise words were soothing. "I have an hour free now, I will sit with you and after you drink will take you to the staff shower room, you will feel a little better when you have washed and changed again" she said. "Thank you," he replied.

The sergeant did background checks on both Martin and Bret, neither of them had ever been in trouble with the police before and all reports showed legitimate hard-working businessmen. Martin was allowed a phone call and he rang Kay, he told her everything that had happened She was distraught and told him she'd catch the next train out to Little Hampton.

Destiny Rose

In one of the operation theatres in the hospital a Surgeons shouted. "WE NEARLY LOST HIM, BUT HIS PULSE IS BACK."

The damage to Bret's brain was catastrophic and they were lucky to have gotten his pulse back. There was no doubt that he was braindead, the life support machine would keep him alive, and they needed him to stay alive because they needed one of his internal organs to save the life of a young lady who had just been rushed in with a medical emergency. The lady had a damaged lung and waiting lists for transplants were long, some people waited years, she needed one right now and was lucky a perfect match could be found so quick. They would contact his next of kin and take instructions.

Martin's mobile phone was in the Sergeant's desk drawer and it started to ring. He answered the call and he was surprised to hear the hospital doctor on the other end. He explained he'd got Martin's number off Bret's phone with Martin being the person he had called the most. Then told him about the situation at the hospital.

'Martin was Bret's next of kin they had sorted it out years ago. If anything was to happen to either of them, the other would take control of their affairs'

The sergeant opened a little window on the door. "The hospital has rung your phone" he said. Martin stood up. "Is he dead??" he asked. The sergeant told him Bret was brain-dead, but she was hanging on to by a thread then told him the hospital needed to find his next of Kin. "I am his next of kin, he has no-one else, but why do they need the next of kin?" Martin said. "I am not sure; they will explain when we get there." The Sergeant said and rang the doctor back.

Martin remained silent all the way to the hospital and when they arrived a doctor was waiting for them. They took him to a private room and offered a chair to sit down on, but whatever it was, Martin decided that he wanted to hear it standing up. The doctor explained the situation, and he ended by saying. "We need your written permission to give Mr. David's lung to Laura. Martin's legs swayed beneath him, it was all too much to take in and he put his hands on the chair to steady himself. Sergeant Johnson advised Martin to sit down and he did. Then he said. "You can make this right you can save her life." Martins head was spinning all over the place, he looked at the doctor., "You' are asking me to take away the tiny bit of life" he has left, to end his life?" he replied. "He is brain-dead there will be no recovery for him, without the life support he would die within an hour. Your friend's life cannot be saved but Laura's can?" The Doctor said. Martin looked helplessly at the Sergeant, their eyes locked for a moment, then Martins head began to spin, he felt as though his brain was swirling around in a tornado of blood and he could see Bret and Laura's lifeless bodies on the floor in that cove. The colour drained from his face and he was sick. The nurse and Sergeant immediately started to clean up Martin and the mess,

"can I see him please? Martin asked.

"Yes, I will come with you" the Sergeant replied.

The doctor led the way and upon entering the room Martin could barely see Bret because of all the machines and wires surrounding him. He walked closer to his bed, he was wearing a silver metal helmet and his face was covered with a medical mask. Martin knew that thing on his head was holding whatever brain he had left together, Martin touched his hand, he felt as cold as a block of ice, and he couldn't hear him breathing he was so quiet. Martin had never heard him this quiet before, even

Destiny Rose

when he slept, he snored a little, but here in front of him, there was nothing, nothing but a deathly silence and machines dinging and beeping and making the noises. It was over for Bret and Martin knew it, he took hold of his hand, kissed it gently and said, "rest now my brother, my friend, until we meet again." He looked at the doctor, his voice was barely a whisper, "take whatever you need just save her life please." He said. Immediately the doctor handed him a consent form which he signed.

This was a day Martin would never forget, it was a miracle Laura was still alive and to save her he had to end the little shred of existence on this earth Bret had. He would never forget this day the last day for him and Bret, just like he would never forget the first day they met too. After a few minutes, they all left the room and as the door shut behind them and Martin got a shiver up his spine. He felt like he had left Bret to die alone in that room. He would make sure that he had a decent burial. Martin asked the Sergeant if he could ring Kay, the sergeant nodded.

Ray stayed in the hospital overnight, sleeping in the chair in the family room. The doctor woke him at 6am to tell him that Laura was out of theatre and settled in the intensive care unit, then he explained how she would be given various medications over the next few days, to help her body accept and cope with the new organ. Ray wouldn't be allowed to visit her for a few days, but could still stay in the hospital, until he could see her. Jenny the nurse said she would find him somewhere more suitable to sleep

Ray went home to collect a few items and dropped in on Marcy, she thought he looked pale and made him some dinner, he ate the lot he didn't realise just how hungry he had been, he told her that Laura had a little operation and she was recovering well, he didn't want to traumatize her with the full extent of what happened, not yet, and although gossip travelled fast around the village, he was sure he had a week or two, before the news about what happened would get around'

It was 2pm when he arrived back at the hospital.

CHAPTER ELEVEN --- HOPE

Kay arrived in Little Hampton at 3.30pm, she had spoken to the Sergeant on the phone, he was deeply concerned for Laura and allowed her half an hour's visit with Martin, he told her usually he would have refused him a visit but, on this occasion used his discretion, he also informed her that Martin would be kept in police custody as an accessory to attempted murder...

No physical contact was allowed he talked to her through the window in his cell door, he told her everything, she was distraught at the news, and thankful that Martin had not been hurt. The thought of Laura fighting for her life left her heartbroken.

"She will survive, she has to," Kay said, tears streaming down her face, "she will, I'm sure of it Kay" he replied, then he reached his hand out of the window and gently stroked her cheek. The sergeant saw his hand reach out, but kept silent, and before Kay left the station, the sergeant advised her to stay away from the village, explaining that when people found out about what happened to Laura, they may point the finger at her, he gave her a phone number to a guesthouse in the next village, Kay thanked him.

Three days later and 7pm couldn't come quick enough for Ray, he would see Laura for the first time, he had kept Kay up to date with her progress and arranged for her to be able to see Laura for a short time after his visit.

Destiny Rose

Everybody had decided not to tell Laura anything about who the organ donor was, they all thought the decision was in her best interest. Her body had accepted the new lung and the doctors were pleased with her progress.

Ray was nervously waiting, then the doctor and nurse came to take him to Laura's room.

Laura was recovering in a private room, the nurse entered first followed by the doctor and then Ray saw her, she was lay down but awake and she smiled, he rushed to her side, she looked pale, but she was okay, 'thank God'. "Hi," he said and bent down and gave a gentle kiss on her cheek. "Hi, it is so nice to see you," she said, he looked exhausted, "you look worse than me." she joked. Ray strained a smile. "Don't worry anymore Ray, it's going to be okay now, I just know it is," she said. Tears filled Ray's eyes at the sound of her words, even though she was the one in pain she was trying to comfort him, but he refused to cry, instead he stayed strong, he would stay strong for her she deserved no less, "Yes, everything will be okay now he repeated, then the nurse brought him a chair to sit down on. He was careful were he set the chair because she had so many machines and wires around her, once settled he took hold of her hand.

The Doctor checked Laura was fine and then left the room, the nurse stayed and sat on a chair in the corner of the room.

Laura told Ray the last thing that she remembered was Martin trying to stop Bret from shouting at her, and after that, she remembered nothing, but as soon as she woke up, they informed her about the operation. Then she said. "It is sad to think that I am alive only because somebody who was a donor had died."

"Yes, it is, we must thank the doctors, they have been amazing" he said. Then he told her how Charlie had led him to her, Laura smiled.

"What a good boy he is, and how is Marcy?" Ray explained that he hadn't told her the full story nor the extent of her injuries

Destiny Rose

yet, but he would. Laura smiled at the idea of Charlie rescuing her. Then Laura said. "When he was shouting at me, I wasn't scared of what he might do to me, I was in fear of him finding out about you" then she went quiet. Ray said, I wish that animal had found me before you - I've never felt as helpless as I have these last few days." She gave a smile. "I'm still here, so you can stop worrying as much now, but I have to admit that when I first woke up with all these machines around me, I thought I had been abducted by aliens and was on a spaceship!" Ray laughed, then said. "I should never have let you walk through those woods on your own, I should have anticipated that crazy man would come looking for you" Laura squeezed his hand a little.

"It's not your fault for letting me walk through the woods, nor my fault for visiting Marcy. It is Bret's fault. He did this to me, he is to blame not you or me," he knew she was right, and he lifted her hand to his lips, and kissed it gently. Then she said, "I hope he is in custody?" Ray turned away from her gaze. 'She didn't know he was dead, so she mustn't know that he turned the gun on himself, what was he going to say to her?' She noticed Ray's hesitation. "They have him locked up; don't they Ray? "He will never hurt you again Laura, so forget him now and just recover." he replied, she felt sure there was something wrong and then her thoughts went to Martin. "Martin was shouting, he was so angry with him, how is he, please tell me he didn't shoot him too?" He was quick to ease her fears and then someone knocked on the door. The nurse opened it and Kay walked into the room, as soon as she saw Laura she rushed to her bedside and cried out.

"What has he done to you, what has he done?" she was unable to stop her tears from flowing, and she bent gave Laura a gentle hug. Laura was pleased to see her.

"I'm fine Kay I really am," she assured her. The nurse explained that she could only have one visitor in the room at a time. Kay looked at Ray,

"I'm sorry, you must be Ray." He said "hi", then told her to stay for a while, he would come back in ten minutes." He gently kissed Laura then left the room.

"How is Martin? Laura asked. Kay told her Martin would stay in custody until they knew what his part in it was. "But he wasn't involved he tried to stop Bret."

"When you are better, you can tell the police everything you remember, they just want the truth Laura, now forget about Martin he is fine." Then Laura said. "Can't you tell the police for me Kay, they might let him out? Kay took hold of Laura's hand and gently kissed it. "You are worrying about everybody, and they are worrying about you" she said, and then changed the subject. She told her how she and Martin had gotten close and how she felt about him and then wanted to know all about Ray?" Laura told her how they met and felt about each other. "It must have been fate" Kay replied. Laura believed that to. Then Laura said. "Bret, what about Bret?" Kay looked puzzled.

"Who cares what happens to him, the hospital will bury his body, it's not our responsibility?" she replied. "Bury him, is he dead Kay, what happened to him?"

Laura was taken by surprise. The nurse walked over to her bedside and said, "yes Laura, the culprit turned the gun on himself after he shot you, we did everything we could, but we couldn't save him." Kay felt terrible, she didn't know that Laura hadn't been told. The nurse eased her mind and told her it was okay.

Kay knew not to mention who the donor was, but she thought someone would have told her before now he was dead. She looked at Laura, "I am so sorry, I thought you knew?" "It's ok, I know now why Ray felt awkward at my questioning just before you came in. Kay's tears began to fall. Laura continued, "Don't cry, at least Martin is okay, Bret could have shot him so let's be thankful for something. I'm so pleased for you and Martin; you deserve some happiness Kay and so do I. Bret caused all this hurt and I pray he has now found true peace." Then she went quiet. They held each other's hand and stayed silent, then Ray came back. Kay looked at him and said. "I'm sorry Ray, I have taken all your time up" "It's okay, it's nice that you came so quickly, Laura has told me a lot about you, I'm sure your visit has done her the world of good."

"It sure has" Laura replied. The nurse allowed Ray another 10minutes with Laura and both she and Kay left the room to give them privacy for the last few minutes. Kay waited in the corridor for Ray to leave the room, she explained how she told Laura about Bret's death. Ray was happy to hear she had taken the news well, he wasn't upset at the slip, in fact he felt relieved knowing that she knew so she wouldn't have to worry about him or hear his name uttered ever again. Kay then told him how Martin had tried to stop Bret from hurting Laura. Ray didn't reply, remaining silent, he started to walk back to the family room, Kay followed him. "I understand you are angry at Martin, but he isn't the bad one, Bret is, Martin was trying to stop him doing anything bad" she said.

Ray stopped walking and turned to face her. "Laura thinks a lot of you, but I don't know you very well. I'm sure you're a nice person, but I suggest you stop trying to defend that man to me. He should have rung the police as soon as that lunatic found out where Laura was, he must have known what he was capable of" he snapped. Kay was silent for a few seconds and then said,

"what Bret did was totally out of character Martin had never known him to carry a gun" and before she could utter another word, Ray interrupted.

"You are making excuses for his part in what happened. Now, I will ask you politely to stop mentioning their names to me. I've never been a violent man, but right at this moment mentioning their names isn't doing my temperament any good when truthfully, I just want to strangle the life out of the pair of them. One of them I can never get my hands on, but the other, don't tempt me!"   Tears filled her eye's she felt awful. "I'm really sorry, please forgive me for being so insensitive," she shouted out then rushed to the exit. He heard her apology and knew she didn't mean any harm, but he needed to let her know, he just wasn't ready to hear some things at this moment in time.

Laura was angry at Bret, and a little part of her felt sorry for him too, his mind must have been must have been in turmoil to do what he did, but even though he was dead she would never forgive him. He tried to kill her, but hadn't succeeded, and she was thankful that she'd survived. Now she had a chance at life again and would concentrate fully on her future with Ray, then she fell into a deep and peaceful sleep.

The following morning Kay visited Martin and told him what Laura had said. Martin was happy to hear Laura was recovering well and felt relieved she knew that he didn't know what Bret was going to do and was capable of.

Ray spent most of the day reading in the family room, he could visit Laura at 1pm and 7pm for an hour.   He'd arranged with Kay for her to have the first 15 minutes of the visit.   At 12.30pm, Kay walked into the room and she gave a smile. "Hope you managed to get some sleep last night, you must be shattered staying in the hospital all the time?" she said and sat down a few seats away from him. Ray looked at her. "Not really, they wheel a hospital bed in here for me at night and they are not the comfiest of things to sleep on but it's better than the chair, how about you?" She looked at him and with sincerity in her eyes she said, "I haven't slept much since the day they left the City looking for her. It's been the worst time of my life, I was worried about Laura and Martin" she said, then lowered her head and went quiet. "Why didn't you ring the police and warn them he was looking for her?" he asked. Kay thought for a moment, and with honesty told him that ringing the police had never crossed her mind. Martin always had the upper hand over Bret physically and mentally and was sure he could control the situation. Ray reflected on her words then said.

"He may have had the upper hand physically and mentally over a man who was sane and rational, but let's face it, her husband was none of those things. She told me what he's done to her over the years, so how can you think one person can control someone who is totally unbalanced? People like him are never predictable." Then he retreated into silence. He didn't want to make Kay feel like he was blaming her. He was just angry at how wrong it all was. Kay knew he was right and maybe if she had stepped into the middle of Laura's marriage, it could have changed things, then Kay said. "She told me she wanted to leave him, and I helped her. If she'd asked me years ago, I would have done the same. I think she was determined to help him change, but you are right, I should have done something sooner. I truly am sorry and thank God she's okay." Ray gave her a smile then said.

"Sometimes nothing we do is ever enough to change some people, and we cannot change the past, but we will learn from it, and I'm sure we will" he said, Kay nodded. He was a wise and caring man and Kay was happy that Laura had found him, she would be safe with him. Shortly after their chat Kay went to see Laura.

Two week later and Laura could go home, she was recovering extremely well. The doctor was amazed by her progress most people felt weak and a little sick for the first few weeks after such a major operation, but Laura was the opposite. Ray was just happy that they were finally going home. An aftercare and rehabilitation package were in place which meant regular visits from nurses, and a team of physiotherapists would help her over the next few months. The team had already set up some heart and blood pressure monitoring equipment up in Ray's bedroom. The drive from the hospital was a relief for them both. Ray thought he was the luckiest man alive to have her beside him after all she'd been through. He looked at her as she sat quietly in the passenger seat and she spotted him glancing her way. She smiled, then, as if she had read his thoughts she said. "I can't believe I'm sat here beside you and we are going home, when I was being taken, I was afraid I would never see you again."

He kept his eyes on the road and replied, "when I saw you lay on that sand, my world fell apart and there was nothing I could do." She looked at him, "Maybe there really is somebody up there, watching over us Ray" and she pointed up to the sky.

She felt somebody had helped her come back from the brink of death so she could be sat beside him now and he felt it was their destiny to meet, and the love they felt for each other would keep them strong. He looked at her smiled then looked up and replied.

"Perhaps there is"

Marcy had made soup and was waiting for them to arrive home and as soon as their car pulled up, she rushed out to greet them. She broke down crying at the sight of Laura, she was so pleased to see her back home and hugged her gently.

Ray told Marcy the full story about Bret, the shooting and the transplant too. Marcy's heart broke at the news but hearing she was making a fantastic recovery helped her to come to terms with it all. A nurse had spoken to Marcy about how best to help Laura during the recovery process and over the next few weeks

Destiny Rose

Marcy would get as much information as possible for them all to read over regarding recovering after a major organ transplant.

Laura was delighted to see Marcy; she'd missed her, Ray took the bags then went into the house, she had already set up the kitchen table for them both to have something to eat. Afterwards Ray had put their belongings away, Marcy made a pot of tea. Laura was relieved to be home It felt so nice to be sitting in comfort again, Ray sat next to her on the sofa. Marcy placed the tea tray on the coffee table then sat in Ray's armchair. She looked at Ray and Laura and let out a huge sigh of relief,

"Thank Goodness, Thank Goodness and that is all I have to say" she said. Ray and Laura totally understood her sentiment and felt the same! Ray poured them all a drink and in silence for the first time in weeks they each enjoyed their drink.

Over the next few weeks, Laura got stronger, she got closer to Marcy, making them more like a mother and daughter than just friends. Marcy and Charlie visited her every day. The nurses came often, and all was going smoothly. Ray had suggested that he could build a replica of Marcy's cottage in their own back garden it would save her having to walk through the woods. At first the ladies thought it was such a big project to take on, but Ray convinced them, saying it would be brilliant if Marcy could open her front door and just be a stone's throw away and Charlie could run up and down from one house to the other.

The Sergeant took a signed statement from Laura on the third day at home. The gun was retrieved from the cove and after a few days Martin was released. Kay stayed in the rented room and Martin joined her, she didn't want to go back to the city, not until Laura's aftercare at home was finished and she didn't need it anymore. Martin would travel back and forth from the city to the motel. Ray would never forgive Martin for what happened to Laura but had promised her he would be hospitable towards him for her sake. Ray, Kay, and Martin had agreed never to mention Bret's name again.

Laura continued to recover and would be signed off the aftercare services list within the next fortnight, but there was something worrying her, she had been suffering headaches for a fortnight with a severe stabbing pain to one side of her head. She didn't want to tell anyone about it not even Kay. She wanted her to be able to go back home and start to enjoy her life with martin and wanted a bit of normality back in all their lives...

CHAPTER TWELVE --- VISIONS

Two weeks later, 1am and everyone in Little Hampton was asleep except Laura. Laura was standing in the cove in the exact same place Bret had tried to take her life, her eyes were wide open, but her mind was wide asleep. Trancelike standing at the water's edge, staring out into the darkness then suddenly the cold sea water splashed around her feet and she woke up, and immediately knew where she was.

'What the hell was she doing here?' her mind cried out. Her dressing gown was torn at the ends, slippers covered in mud and she was shivering with the cold, she ran as fast as she could to get away from this horrible place and back to her home. The house was in in darkness, but the front door was wide open, she took her slippers off and holding them walked into the hallway. There was nothing but silence around her, Ray must still be asleep, so quietly she went to the bathroom put her dirty clothes in the bottom of the wash basket and covered them with some towels, then cleaned herself, put a fresh night clothes on and went downstairs to make a hot chocolate.

What the hell had happened to her, she had never walked in her sleep before? Why did she go to that dreadful place? a place that she never wanted to see again, she sat on the sofa and sipped her drink. First, the headaches and now this, she wanted to run up the stairs and tell Ray, she felt sure he would know what to do and understand what was happening to her, but something stopped her. For some reason her instinct told her to keep it to herself, Ray had been treating her like a china doll for quite a while now and it was lovely however, she just wished that they could go back to the way they were before that terrible night, she finished her drink then went to bed.

The next morning 7am, Ray looked at Laura while she slept, then kissed her softly on the cheek, she opened her eyes, smiled and replied by giving him a longer kiss. Then he said, "I love you so much." Laura loved him too; he was the best thing that had ever happened to her, he was her hero, as well as her best friend. Ray slipped his arm around her waist and pulled her closer. They kissed passionately, and Laura wanted more, she wanted to feel every inch of him. His heart was beating fast, and his mind was lost in some wonderful, peaceful place. His body was aching to feel her every inch and throbbing to be inside her. He had missed this closeness, but suddenly he dropped his hold and pulled away.

"I'm sorry, I need to take a shower," he said, then left the room. She watched him leave, she knew why he was holding his feelings back. He was worried about her surgery, but it had been such long time, and she missed the intimacy they shared before that night.

Ray left for work at 10am; he had returned but just for a few hours each day. Marcy was going on a day trip with some of the locals from the village, so Laura decided after taking Charlie a walk she would ring Kay, she would ask her advice about sleepwalking!

At 11am she walked into the cottage and was met by an excited Charlie! His tail wagged, and he jumped up at her boisterously, his front paws landed on her chest, and he started licking her face. Laura laughed and pushed him down, she calmed him by stroking his head gently then they headed into the woods. They didn't venture far, Charlie sniffed at the ground with each step he took, she let him off the lead and strolled along watching him as he rushed in and out of the trees in hope of glimpsing another animal, so he could give chase. Then suddenly the pain in the side of her head started again, she rubbed her temple and closed her eyes for a minute, but the pain didn't go, she opened her eyes and froze at the sight of a man staring down at her and standing directly in front of her, he was tall possibly 7 ft., she looked up at his face, his cold ice blue eyes stared right into hers, his face was long and thin, wrinkles and lines came down his cheeks, from his eyes to the side of his mouth, his grey wiry hair was heavily greased back over his head and although his eyes were like the colour of ice his stare was cold and dark. They stared at each other then suddenly everywhere around them went black. There were no trees, no Charlie, nothing but blackness and she shouted out,

"What is happening, who are you, move out of my way?" The man stepped closer, she raised her hand to push him backwards, then she noticed that her own hand was small like that of a young child. It didn't look like her hand. She looked down and her feet were small too and she was wearing boy's shoes.? What on earth was happening to her? was she losing her mind?" Then suddenly the man reached out and gripped her shoulder and purposely dug his fingers into her shoulder-bone, she screamed out in pain. Then he said. "I have been looking for you, for such a long time. His teeth were yellow and broken, he terrified her, she continued to scream then she heard Charlie barking and he jumped up at her and the man had vanished? Everything around her was back to normal now, her hands were her own hands now and so was her feet and she felt sick. What on earth was happening to her, something was terribly wrong… Laura took Charlie back to Marcy's then went home, she couldn't keep this to herself she would have to confide in Kay, there was no-one else she could talk to about it and she didn't want to explain everything over the phone, so they arranged for Kay to come to her.

Kay listened as Laura recounted her recent experiences. The headaches, sleepwalking and now this vision of that horrible man. Kay didn't know what to say because she couldn't think of any reason why these things were happening. "Maybe you should tell Ray" she said. But Laura explained how he was already treating her like a fragile piece of porcelain, and she didn't want to add to that. Kay assured her she would help and suggested they visit a library and try to find some books with information of why people might start hallucinating, and if that didn't help, she would have to ask a doctor.
"Thank you, I knew you would know what to do" Laura said and hugged her. Kay was happy to help she knew a problem shared was a problem halved and agreed to keep this between themselves. Kay wondered if Laura was suffering some form of delayed shock and may have post-traumatic stress disorder, but she didn't say anything. She would try and find out what the symptoms were. Laura felt a little weight lift from her shoulders. Kay returned to the motel. Martin had arrived back earlier he had been to Deminick for a few days. When she walked in he joked," you left me, and I have missed you so much, you don't care about me anymore" Kay smiled, "well I'm back now and you have my undivided attention" she said, he slipped his hand around her waist and pulled her close. 'Do I tell you enough just how much I love you?" he whispered. Kay giggled, and replied, "Yes, you do but if you want to show me how much, then that's okay with me," and giggled again. Martin swept her up into his arms, and kissing her, carried her into the bedroom, their lovemaking as always was beyond their imagination. Every-time they came together they would discover

Destiny Rose

new ways to please each other, each time it felt like they had created a masterpiece of love.

Marcy rung Ray early in the evening to tell them how her day had gone, she also told them about a friend named Tom who was 70 years old. They had gotten close over the last few months and like her was a regular church goer.

They had known each other for years, he was born and raised in the village too. He was a keen fisherman and she would love for them both to meet him one day. Then she told Ray about buying a book in an old curiosity shop. The book was about the children's home where she worked as a nurse in her late teens. Ray told her to bring Tom over to meet him, and bring the book too, they could all look at it together. She told him she would bring them tomorrow. That night when Laura undressed to take a bath, she caught her reflection in the mirror, there was a black and blue bruise on her shoulder. It was in the same place the man in the woods had grabbed her. She closed her eyes not wanting to look at it. It couldn't be that man because she was sure he didn't exist. Maybe she had banged it and just forgot?

Marcy had a busy day walking around the shops, she was sat in her chair by the fire with Charlie at her feet. She picked up the book she had bought from the shop, the title read. 'Allonywood children's home'. She wanted to read it, but was too tired, she put it down and slowly drifted off to sleep.

The next day Ray went into work, in the afternoon, Marcy dropped in on Laura, Kay was there too. The ladies sat at the kitchen table. Marcy told them about working in a children's home as a nurse many years ago and she showed them the book. Kay flipped through it looking at the images mostly, then passed it to Laura. She looked through it, then suddenly froze at the sight of a picture. It was a black and white print of a group of

Destiny Rose

workers from the home and one man stood out to her. He looked younger in this picture, but it was him, the same man she saw in the woods just a few days ago, his face was etched in her mind. she would never forget those cold and piercing eyes. The description under the picture read, Mr. Surringer, and the name sent a shiver down her spine. Laura looked at Kay and then too Marcy who were both chatting, her eyes focused on the name Surringer and it started to swirl around her mind. Then everything around her became blurred and suddenly she felt sick?

"I will make a fresh pot of tea" she shouted out, Marcy and Kay looked at her , " we already have a fresh brew, dear Marcy said, but with the book in her hand Laura walked towards the kettle, then suddenly she fainted and fell to the floor. The book skidded across the room. Kay jumped up from her seat.

"Laura, Laura are you okay?" she shouted and knelt beside her, she was unconscious. "Ambulance Marcy, we need an ambulance" Marcy rang for an ambulance and then Ray walked through the door. "What's happened?" he shouted out and the colour drained from his face, they explained, then heard the siren outside. The nurse took her pulse then tried smelling salts to wake her, but it didn't work.

Destiny Rose

CHAPTER THIRTEEN --- MEMORIES

Ray and Marcy travelled to the hospital in the ambulance. Tom would be coming to Ray's soon, so Kay stayed behind, and would tell him what had happened, then she rang Martin. In the hospital Ray and Marcy waited for news about Laura, they'd not heard a thing since the ambulance crew rushed her in an hour ago.

Ray sat in silence with his head in his hands, but he was slowly losing his patience.

"Why haven't they come to talk to us yet. They could at least let us know that she's okay?" His face was a mask of desperation. Marcy had never seen him so worked up. She didn't like seeing him so desperate and scared and not being able to help him. "I will go and find someone who can give us some answers; you stay here in case the doctor comes." "Okay" he said, he couldn't believe they were back in the hospital again. He stared at the waiting room door, wanting Laura to walk through it, so they could all go home, but a little voice inside his head said that wasn't going to happen. Something was wrong, why else were they being left here like this? Then the doctor walked into the room with Marcy she sat down next to Ray and held her head down low. The doctor was the same man who had looked after Laura last time.

"Something is wrong, what is it, just tell me?" Ray said desperately. The doctor explained that Laura's mind for some reason had shut itself down. Ray didn't understand what he was saying, "What do you mean shut down. I don't understand.

Destiny Rose

"Mr. Maitland, up to now we can only suggest it is some sort of mental breakdown" Tears fell down Marcy's cheeks, she looked at Ray and said "Maybe she just needs a rest after all she has been through, she will get through this I am sure of it Ray." The doctor told him, that people could come out of these episodes within hours, or a few days, and that they would keep Laura in hospital for as long as it takes for her to be well again.

Ray couldn't believe this was happening, but he would stay strong, he had to for her, he asked if he could see Laura and the doctor led them both to her room, she was hooked up to machines again but looked peaceful and as beautiful as always, he held her hand, "my angel, I am so sorry I didn't stop this from happening," he said. Marcy put her arm around Ray's waist and told him that there was nothing he could have done, but he was in deep turmoil and she could see it. After a few minutes the doctor led them back to the waiting room. Ray sat down, he looked like a little boy lost and her heart was breaking seeing him so vulnerable, he would ring Kay soon to ask Martin if he would bring him an overnight bag and pick Marcy up, he would be staying in hospital again Ray wanted to stay near Laura, and the hospital had no problem with that. Tears were streaming down Kay's face when Martin arrived,

"Martin, it's awful" she cried out and sobbed uncontrollably. Martin held her and led her to the sofa, and they sat in silence for a few minutes, he was holding her close while she was breaking down. "I should have told him, I should have told him what was going on, maybe if I had said something, this wouldn't have happened."

Martin didn't have a clue what she was talking about, "told who what, Kay you are not making any sense?" he said, she lowered her head and fell silent. Gently he put his fingers under her chin and turned her face to his.

"Kay, what do you mean, what is it?" Then she told Martin about Laura's headaches, the sleepwalking and lastly the visions. It took a few seconds for what she'd said to register. "Yes, you should have spoken to him Kay, or at least me. You really should have, but this isn't your fault, you couldn't have foreseen what would happen, and no-one could have prevented this, I'm sure it helped her that you knew what she was going through, at least she wasn't going through it alone" he reassured her. Then he continued. "It could be delayed shock, she may snap out of it later or tomorrow, but if she doesn't then we need to talk to the doctor to tell him what has been happening to her, it may help them help her. "

"Oh Martin, thank you, I feel so bad, but she didn't want anyone else to know, and I promised her I wouldn't tell anyone," she said, her sob's easing. Martin held her for a while then went to make a warm drink. As he was walking back to the living room near the kitchen door he spotted the book on the floor, he looked down at it and he froze as he read the large golden lettered title 'Allonywood children's home' he put the drinks down on the kitchen table and picked the book up. "Kay where did this come from? "he asked, holding the book up, and she explained it was Marcy's, she had worked there as a nurse when she was younger. He put the book down on the table making sure the title wasn't facing him, and he thought, 'how strange that out of all the places, Marcy worked in that one?'.... He walked into the living room and immediately Kay noticed he looked a little pale.

"Is everything okay?" she asked, he sat beside her on the sofa.

"Yes, I just had a shock seeing that book that's all, "he replied.

"Laura was reading that book just before she fainted, do you know that place Martin?" she asked. Martin had no reason to lie and explained Allonywood was the home where he and Bret first met and a place, they both were happy to forget.

Destiny Rose

(He kept anything to do with the abuse out of the conversation) Kay changed the subject and shocked him by saying, "Martin I'm pregnant, I was taking the pill, but I missed a couple of tablets I am sorry" Martin looked at her, he couldn't believe it. "Sorry, why sorry. It's amazing Kay, it's the best news ever." he put his arm around her and kissed her, she felt relieved that he was as happy as she was. "I'm going to be a dad. I can't believe it and you a mummy" he said excitedly. Kay smiled and told him the doctor had confirmed it a few days ago, she was eight weeks pregnant, she was waiting for the right time to tell him, and although this wasn't the best of times she didn't want to keep it from him. Then she asked him if they could keep it a secret between them both while Laura was in hospital and that when she was better and home, they could share the news with them all them. Martin agreed, he looked at Kay and said. "She will love being an aunty "Kay smiled, "Yes she will, please God let her be well and home soon." she replied.

At 3pm Tom knocked on the door. Immediately Kay told him what happened, and that Martin was going to pick Marcy up and take Ray an overnight bag in half an hour. Then she went to make a pot of tea. Tom followed her into the kitchen and sat down at the table, he picked the book up. "Marcy's book?" he said. Kay turned to him. "Yes, how strange how Martin lived in that place when he was little years after Marcy worked there, what are the chances of that?" "I would say a one in a billion chance" Tom replied. Then Martin asked Tom if Marcy had talked about the home to him. Tom knew nothing, "but, her mood seemed to go low after she found it, like a weight had been placed on her shoulders as soon as we left the shop. I don't know why?" he said. Martins mood was low too, but he knew why…. Kay asked them if they wanted a sandwich, Tom

Destiny Rose

accepted, Martin refused, then said he would go and pick Marcy up. Kay had already sorted Ray an overnight bag and Martin left.

As Laura lay in the hospital bed, all everybody around her could see was a young lady who looked like she was sleeping, but although her eyes were closed, her mind was wide awake, and nobody would see over the next few days that her thoughts would go into complete turmoil. Visions of places and people, some she knew but had forgotten, and some who she had never known, images and memories would invade and over-load her and some of those memories were not her own, they were Bret's. Little did she or anyone else know that when she received his lung, not only had his blood slowly pumped through her veins, somehow like in other rare cases noted in the world, his memories had found a way to into her mind.

Cellular memory transference is the idea that memories or characteristics of an organ donor can be passed on and into the organ recipient, and although an unproven fact, it really does exist because it was happening to Laura right now.

The first memory she had was one of her own, she was three years-old and lying in her bed. It was early in the morning and the bedroom door flung open, and her father walked in shouting at her.

"Get up, get up quick, or I'll slap the hide off you, do you hear!" Laura scrambled out of bed, her father picked up her pillow and placed a handgun underneath it. Then he told her to lie back down, and her not to say a word no matter who came into the room or she would be in trouble. Pretend to be asleep" he demanded. Then he covered her with her blanket, she didn't want to make him angrier, then she heard a stranger's voice talking to her Father, he was ordering him to go into the other bedrooms, and then they were stood outside her room. "What's in here?" she heard a stranger's voice ask. "My daughter is in there and she is asleep, so leave the room alone." her father replied.

The policeman glanced at her and left the room, and only when her dad returned and spoke to her did, she open her eyes, he took the gun and left. Laura lay in bed listening to her mother and father shouting at each other downstairs. The front door slammed, then her mother rushed up the stairs. "Aren't you dressed yet. Get your clothes on and hurry up, we're going out!" she yelled. She dressed quickly, having no time to wash, brush her hair, clean her teeth, or have any breakfast, an and followed her mother to a friend's house. They stayed there until the pub opened and remained there all day till it closed. Laura watched people drink, smoke, talk, and swear all day, she was lucky sometimes and managed to get a glass of orange juice, a packet of crisp's and some other bits of food from customers during the day. This was a normal day for her, if she wasn't in the pub it was somebody's house for the day and if she had the opportunity she would play with other kids.

(Laura had no recollection of what her parents looked like, but these visions had shown her exactly what they looked like and who they were)

Her mother was terribly thin and deeply wrinkled, she was 30 years old but looked like an old lady. Her hair was mousey brown, short and limp. He teeth were rotted and bad, years of smoking and drinking had taken their toll. Laura was nothing like her mother. Her father had dark hair and eyes, a moustache and beard he was short, fat, bald and a thief who would steal from anyone, houses, shops, nothing was safe from him, he would even rob old people or a church, he would pick peoples pocket's and got away with it. and Laura refused to call him dad.

Destiny Rose

Laura was dragged from pillar to post and knew no different, she thought every home was like this; and it was only when she started school at 5 years of age, that people were concerned at the apparent signs of neglect. The teachers began asking questions about the little girl who'd recently joined their school.

Life set out for Laura under the care of her parents was destined to be a bad one, but one teacher was determined that wasn't going to happen, she contacted the local authorities and after a thorough investigation. The authorities were quick to act and a few days later they arrived to take her into their care. On the morning the authorities arrived to conduct Laura's removal, her mother's last words were, "Good riddance, nothing but a ball and chain around my neck that child has been." Mrs. Taylor, the teacher kept in touch with the services looking after her, keeping a check on her progress.

The vision in Laura's mind was like she was watching a short video clip on you tube. It was clear and descriptive but fleeting, and when the clip was over, most of the content/memory would vanish from her mind, but parts would remain forever.

The second vision Laura saw, was of a young boy, he was about 8 years old, sat on a bench in a field with nothing but more fields for miles? His hair was dark and curly, he was holding the strings of a bunch of coloured balloons. The strings were long, and the balloons danced around high up in the wind, but he kept his head low as though he was looking at the ground, she couldn't see his face. he was wearing short trousers up to his knees and his legs were painfully thin they looked as thick as twigs. A deep sadness filled her, she felt sorry for the child and wanted to reach out, to touch him and to let him know that he wasn't alone, and as though he had read her mind the little boy looked at her, their eyes met and he was sure she had seen him before?

Then his mouth opened wide and began to scream, the sound was deafening, it was a piercing scream, she covered her ears and after a few seconds the boy's image disappeared... Laura's mind immediately switched off, and she fell into silence and darkness for a while.

Martin arrived at the hospital. Ray and Marcy were waiting by the main door, she got into the car and the two men stood talking. Ray asked Martin if he and Kay wanted to stay in one of the spare bedrooms in his house, they would be support for Marcy. Martin thought it a good idea, he was happy the women could support each other. Then Ray continued, "I haven't told her your part in what happened to Laura she would never forgive you and could hold it against Kay and I don't want that. I said you came to the village together, but he didn't know what he had planned and had nothing to do with it." Martin thanked him.

"I'm not doing this for you I'm doing it for Marcy, Laura and Kay." he replied, then went back into the hospital.

Destiny Rose

CHAPTER FOURTEEN --- ACCEPTANCE

The doctor told Ray they were unsure why she had fell into this state. "Maybe its post-traumatic stress" Ray replied. The doctor neither agreed nor disagreed. "Let's just take it one day at a time" he said.

Kay was visiting today, and it was noon when she arrived. Ray was dozing on the chair beside Laura's bed when a knock on the door woke him. He looked worn out and gave a strained smile.

"You need a good sleep; you don't want to make yourself ill Ray?" he shook his head.

"No, I can't, I can't sleep not yet" he replied.

"But it will help you stay strong while you're going through this" she said. Ray disagreed, telling her he didn't want to go to sleep in case Laura woke up. Kay reassured him that if she sat with Laura for a couple of hours then he could get some sleep and promised to wake him up immediately if she woke up. Ray agreed but didn't want to leave the room and decided to sleep in another chair in the room, and it wasn't long before he settled into the chair and fell asleep.

Ray woke up at 7 pm. Kay looked at him smiled and said, "she didn't wake up." "Thanks, you were right I did need that sleep" he replied. Then she went to get him a drink of coffee. Martin picked her up at 7.30, he brought sandwiches for Ray that Marcy had made.

The next day, Kay arrived at noon and within the hour Ray fell asleep again in the chair. She started to read a book and after a few minutes, Laura shouted out. "Surringer, Surringer?" Kay stood up, but Laura went silent. Kay gently nudged her arm,

"Laura, Laura, are you awake?" but she didn't move an inch. Ray was still asleep, and she went to find the nurse. The nurse checked the machinery around her bed, there had been no reading that she had woken.

"Maybe you nodded off and dreamt it Kay?" the nurse said, then left the room. Kay knew for sure she didn't fall asleep, and Laura's words were clear in her mind. 'Surringer?' She had never heard that word before. Kay picked her book back up and tried to carry on reading, but she couldn't, something didn't feel right, she put the book down and watched Laura sleeping.

The next day was the same for Kay and Ray but for Laura it wasn't the same at all and there was nothing she could do about it. Her body was paralysed, and she had no choice but to confront the images in her mind. Her mother was angry and standing over her shouted.

"Nightmares! I'll give you nightmares, do you really think I've got time for this, time for you to piss the bed. You want your bedding changed, because you can't be bothered to get up and go to the toilet. You're not a baby, you wet it, so you can bloody well sleep in it. That'll teach you not to do it again, now get back to sleep and don't call me again!" She left the room slamming the door behind her. Then Laura remembered the smell on her mother's breath, she stunk of cigarettes and alcohol. The scene in Laura's mind then suddenly changed and she saw the little boy with dark curly hair again. He was wearing the same clothes and this time he was running fast in a long, dark tunnel. Bizarrely, he was running away from her mother. The boy then turned around and looked directly into Laura's eyes as though he knew she was watching him from her mind. Immediately she recognised it was Bret. Her mother was screaming obscenities at him. Then the tunnel changed into a long dark corridor. Wood

Destiny Rose

panelling covered the tall walls. There were no windows or doorways, then the boy shouted. "Help, somebody please help" but no one came, and her mother continued to chase him down the corridor that seemed to never end, but it did. He reached a solid oak door which was shut, then the door started to open, a hand reached out and dragged the boy inside and the door slammed shut. A man was shouting.

"Where have you been, insolent little rat. What have I told you about being late?" Then Laura saw herself stood in the corridor, but she was young she looked the same age as the boy. Then she heard the boy shout. "No, please no.' she rushed to the door and grabbed hold of the handle, but she couldn't move it, it was stuck solid? The boy continued to shout for help, she had to get in that room somehow. She thumped the door hard.

"Open this door, let me in" she shouted, urgency in her voice. The boy replied, he could not open the door because he wouldn't let him, then Laura started to kick the door.

"Whoever you are, let him out, do you hear me?" but all she heard was the boy whimpering.

"I'm coming don't worry, I will get in there!" and she looked around for anything to hit against the door, but there was nothing, she ran to the other end of the corridor and saw an old iron spiral staircase. Carefully she made it to the bottom and this time it was a wide corridor, with light coming in from the windows and doors along each side, she shouted for help, but no one responded.

"Where is everyone, what is this place?" her mind urged. She rushed to one of the doors, it opened, she stood in the doorway but saw nothing that could help her. The room had at least ten single beds on each side. It was neatly kept, very much like an army barracks but obviously for children. The beds were basic, made of black metal with no headboards. No windows or pictures on the plain white-washed walls, the place sent a shiver up her spine, she shut the door and walked to the door opposite, this turned out to be an old-fashioned gymnasium with polished wooden floorboards and more panelled walls. There was a children's climbing apparatus and floor mats neatly piled up in one corner, and an old church organ against a wall. This room had a large window, she walked over and looked outside. A neatly cut lawn lead up to lots of trees which carried on for as far as she could see. Looking around she knew there was nothing useful in this room.

The next door she opened led into a classroom; it contained a small library against one wall and a projector screen. Then she saw a small hardwood chair, she picked it up and rushed back to the corridor on the top floor. With all her strength, she swung the chair as hard as she could against the doorknob. But no matter how strenuous her efforts the door wouldn't budge. Her arms were beginning to tire, so she stopped for a rest, she was about to resume swinging at the door when the knob started turning. She raised the chair above her head ready to strike if someone threatening appeared. The door slowly opened, and with the chair has her weapon she rushed into the room. Adrenalin was pumping through her, she stood in the middle of the room and looked around but there was no-one in the room. It was completely empty, yet she still felt worried and kept a firm held on the chair.

It looked as though no one had been in the room for years, broken floorboards and cobwebs were hanging from the ceiling, a large desk full of dust sat below a heavily patterned stained-glass window, from the window she could see the whole of the front of the grounds. There was a long driveway leading to a huge rusty gateway and a brick wall at least 7 feet high went around the premises. There was no other furniture in the room, she tried the drawers of the desk, but none of them opened, the only way i out of this room was the door she had come in through. As she put the chair down she noticed a word scraped big and deep into the floorboard, 'HELP' That boy must be in this building somewhere her mind shouted out and quickly she made her way back down the stairs and had got to the bottom rung, then suddenly a tall dark figure stepped into her path stopping her from moving forward.

It was the man she saw in the woods. Then he said, "What do we have here, another little wriggler to whet my appetite?"

(Laura looked like a child to him and not a grown woman) He grabbed hold of her hair and twisted it around his hand. Laura screamed out in pain, kicked him and shouted.

I may look like a child, but I am a grown woman, let go of my hair or I will bite your hand." Then with his other hand he grabbed hold of her shoulder pushing his fingers down as hard as he could into her skin. "Feisty, feral rat, aren't you?" He seethed. Laura sank her teeth into his hand, he cried out and let go of her hair, she managed to twist her way out of his grip and ran away. The man didn't chase her instead he laughed and shouted. "You won't get Bret back if you run away" Laura stopped running,

"Where is he, what have you done with him, let him go" she demanded. He walked slowly towards her and stopped a few feet away. His stare drilled into her. "Don't worry, you're going to find out what happened to him very soon, I am just having a little fun with you." Rage filled her, and she rushed towards him, lashing out, scratching and kicking him. Her foot caught his knee and he lost his footing. He didn't fall but stumbled enough so she could scratch his face.

"You are not invincible you evil, evil man" she shouted, he started to laugh again, she backed away from him, knowing this person in front of her was a deeply disturbed human being.

"where is he, tell me or I will kill you, you monster "she screamed. Laura looked like a child to him; she was no threat at all, he walked towards her, he wanted to shut her up and teach her a lesson.   Laura was ready for him, she wasn't going to run away again, she was going to fight him, he would have to kill her before he'd hurt her, and then ran at him, but suddenly he disappeared and she woke up, she sat up in her hospital bed and was wide awake. Kay was sat on a chair reading. Laura Looked at her and said, "Kay, Kay, what on earth am i doing here?   Kay couldn't believe it, tears welled up in her eyes "oh Laura is that you, are you really awake" she said.   Laura was puzzled. "Yes of course it's me and yes I am awake" The tears continued down Kay's cheeks and she gave her a hug.   "Oh, thank God, you have been asleep for days, we have all been worried sick." Kay told her.   Laura was shocked.   "What on earth happened, I cannot remember anything?" Laura said. Kay told her to hang on and that she would nip out and find a nurse and Ray who, had gone to get a drink.

The nurse and doctor rushed into the room and Kay went to find Ray, she saw him standing at a drinks machine and shouted.

"She is awake, she's awake Ray, he couldn't believe what he was hearing.   "Thank you, thank you Kay" he said, and raced to her room.   Kay continued to cry and finished getting the drinks from the machine.   Relief flooded Ray when he saw her sitting up in the bed and tears filled his eyes, he sat beside her taking hold of her hand.   "I'm so sorry for all that I have put you through Ray" she said, feeling guilty at the anguish he'd suffered worrying about her.

"You have nothing to be sorry for, none of this is your fault" he replied. The doctor told them that the machine readings were normal now, but they would be keeping her in overnight to monitor her progress.   Then left them alone.

"You are a true fighter pulling yourself through, I don't ever want to lose you.   I was just existing before you came into my life, and now I could never imagine being without you." Laura

Destiny Rose

lifted his hand to her mouth and gently kissed it and said. "I feel exactly the same" "This time next year we could get married, if you like?" he said taking her by surprise.

"Yes, yes we can" she said accepting his proposal… Ray smiled and for the first time in ages, she saw a lovely sparkle in his eyes. Tears of happiness rolled down her cheeks, he couldn't believe that just a couple of minutes ago he didn't know if she was ever going to wake up and now he was kissing her and imagining her in a beautiful wedding gown standing next to him. Kay stood in the doorway watching them talking and smiling, it was lovely to see, then went to ring Martin and Marcy…

The next day after tests were completed on Laura, the doctor gave her the all clear. She appeared to be 100%fit, and he decided that whatever had triggered her subconsciousness had now passed.

Kay and Laura were stood in the hospital doorway waiting for Ray to bring the car from the car park. Then Laura said, "Kay there's something I need to tell you" "What is it?" Kay said interrupting, feeling worried. Laura saw fear in her eyes. "It's nothing to worry about, I am okay. It's just that I remember some things from when I was asleep, I must have dreamt them, and I need to talk about them but only to you, is that okay?" Kay put her arm around Laura's waist and holding her she said. "Yes, we can talk but I can't keep it from Martin, you can confide in him, he will be able to help with any problems you have, and Laura I am pregnant? Laura was over the moon at the news and gave Kay a kiss on her cheek. I can't believe it. I am going to be an Aunty; this is just what we all need right now something to look forward too" she said.

CHAPTER FIFTEEN --- THE CALM

Martin, Marcy and Tom were standing at the front door waiting for them to arrive from the hospital. Marcy had set the dining room table and a meal was prepared and ready. As soon as they saw the car making its way up the drive, Marcy rushed out to greet them. During the meal Tom smiled as he watched Marcy fuss over Laura like a mother figure.

After dinner, they sat in the living room, the ladies drank tea and the men decided on wine.

The lady's chatted on the sofa. Ray and Tom relaxed in the armchairs. Martin used a stool from the kitchen to sit on. Marcy was delighted at the news of the pregnancy,

"I must start knitting again I can make the baby some outfits for when 'he or she arrives" she said excitedly. They continued to talk, Marcy kept asking Laura if she was feeling okay and if she wasn't, she must tell her right away, which Kay and Laura found endearing. Marcy then excused herself, wanting to wash the pots and clean up a little. Tom helped her.

Laura invited Kay to join her upstairs saying she could help style her hair. Laura closed the bedroom door and sat on the dressing table chair. Kay began to brush through her hair. Then Laura told her about the visions and memories that she had in hospital, she told her about her mother, father, Bret and Surringer. Kay listened carefully then said. "You shouted that name out twice in hospital, they were the only words you said, I told the nurse, but she said I must have nodded off and dreamt it, who is Surringer Laura, and how do you know him? Kay asked. Laura turned to face Kay. "I don't know him and until I

Destiny Rose

started having these visions, I had never heard the name before. I am not going crazy Kay the visions I had were real" and then she went silent. Kay thought for a moment. "I don't think you are going crazy I believe you. It's okay Laura don't worry about it, I will talk to Martin just give me a few days, he will know what to do" she assured, and continued to brush her hair.

The afternoon passed quickly. Kay and Martin returned to the motel at 6pm. They left Ray's at the same time as Tom and Marcy, and now Ray and Laura were settled on the sofa. "I'm so happy you are home Laura" he said.

"So am I Ray" Then she leant towards him and gave him a loving kiss. He welcomed it and put his arms around her, pulling her closer. The more they kissed, the more she wanted him. it had been a long time since he had swept her up in his arms and carried her upstairs and she wanted that right now, but Ray pulled away and stood up,

"I need a drink; do you want one?" He asked. Laura asked for a glass of white wine. Then said, "Oh, dear I forgot to tell Kay something, I'm just nipping upstairs to get my mobile phone." Ray continued to the kitchen.

Kay was surprised to answer the phone to Laura so soon after leaving their house.

"Kay, I am so sorry to bother you, this isn't anything to do with what we talked about earlier, this is something different." Kay listened as Laura explained how desperate she was for physical interaction with Ray.

"I just don't know what to do Kay" she ended. Martin was sat on the sofa in the room watching the TV. Kay walked into the bedroom and sat down on the bed. "Is everything okay sweetheart?" Martin shouted.

"Yes, everything's fine Martin, we are just having a little chat I won't be long" she replied. Kay thought hard for a moment, then said.

"Let's try and put ourselves in Ray's shoes and imagine how he must be feeling right now. I think it's a confidence issue, he probably thinks you are fragile but if you're not, then… But before Kay could say another word, Laura cried out "Fragile. I don't feel fragile. I was okay as soon as I got home from hospital last time, and I'm okay now. I just need to convince Ray, that I am fine" Kay giggled, "you have both been through a lot, your health is all that matters to him, and the only way to convince him you are okay is by being assertive!!" Laura was puzzled.

"What do you mean by assertive Kay?

"It means you have to take control of the situation and show him the way forward Laura"

"But he's not lost Kay so how can I show him the way when I don't know where it is?" Kay Giggled.

Martin heard her giggling and crept up to the bedroom door and put his ear against it.

"I know he's not lost in a jungle or stuck up a mountain, but he's lost in a different way. He has lost his confidence and you have to get it back for him" Kay replied. Then it dawned on her exactly what Kay meant, because it explained everything about why he was acting the way he was.

"What can I do to help him get that confidence back Kay?" Laura asked.

"Use your imagination Laura, remember when I showed you how to dance in my dressing room all those years ago? Just do that and use your rhythm on him." Kay replied. Laura was shocked at Kays words, "My what? She really couldn't imagine dancing in front of Ray and apart from Kay showing her a little bit of her routine once, she wasn't a good dancer, "but Kay, my

Ray is a gentleman and a nice man, he doesn't want to see me dance…

Kay stopped her mid-sentence and said, "he may be a gentleman, but he's still a red-blooded male Laura, and you are a red hot, bloodied female and he needs you to help him get his sex drive back," Kay told her.

Laura had no idea what she could do to take control of this situation and make it better, so this is what you are going to do and no matter how silly or embarrassed you feel you need to carry it through till the end. Your man needs you to be strong and taking control will get you both one step closer to making it better, it's as simple as that" Kay said. Laura knew this was true, and listened carefully as Kay explained what she should do…

The conversation was over, Kay put the phone down and sighed. She hoped that after tonight Laura and Ray could put the past behind them. Kay opened the bedroom door and was surprised to see Martin standing behind it. He had a big grin on his face. "Well, well, well, my bountiful buxom beauty." He said. Kay knew instantly Martin had overheard the advice she'd given Laura, and she blushed. Then smiled at him. "My dear wife to be, do you want to practice some of those pulsating and rhythmic dance techniques on me? We do have a spare hour you know…" he teased and chuckled. Kay didn't need to be asked twice, she stood on tiptoes, threw her arms around his neck. He whisked her up in his arms and carried her to the bed, Kay's giggles filled the room.

As soon as Laura put the phone down, she opened her negligée drawer to look for the sexiest nightie she possessed, she couldn't see anything which grabbed her; and didn't have any sexy underwear, she felt disappointed. Then she spotted her white lace nightie with a silk lining. Taking it out and holding it up she thought this would be fine. Then she took a pair of scissors and cut the lining completely away from the lace, she put the lining

Destiny Rose

back into the draw then held it up again. This time she smiled - it was perfect! Now she had a nice white sexy see-through lace baby-doll nightie and she rushed excitedly to the top of the stairs and shouted out to Ray that she would be down in 15 minutes, he was happily drinking his wine with his feet up... 'Be assertive, Laura' she kept telling herself, keeping her thoughts fixed on nothing but getting close to Ray again, as close as they were when they first met. Laura dried her hair and put a little makeup on her eyes and lips then put the negligee on, she looked in the full-length mirror in the bedroom and decided she was ready! Then she walked to the top of the stairs and shouted. "Ray, do you fancy an early night, you could bring the wine up here if you like?" He had been so tired over
the last few days and an early night was exactly what he needed.

"Yes, I'll be up in a minute, I will get the wine" he shouted in reply.

Ray held the bottle in one hand and two glasses in the other and made his way to the bedroom, he expected to see Laura, but she wasn't there. Two tall candles lit on the dressing table, they gave the room a cosy glow, he walked to his bedside cabinet put the bottle and glasses down, poured them both a drink, then sat on the bed sipping his wine. "I won't be a minute Ray" She shouted, giving herself one last glance in the bathroom mirror. The nightie stopped at her thighs and clung to her figure perfectly, showing every curve. Her breasts were visible through the lace and her nipples were pert, she chose black lace panties to match the colour of her hair which was hanging loosely down her back, she noticed the scar. It was long but a neat line, it started in the middle of her breasts and went down to the top of her belly button and she worried in case it might put Ray off looking at her, but then Kays' words came to mind. "No matter

Destiny Rose

what, see it through to the end!" and feeling confident she left the bathroom.

Ray was taken by surprise when she walked into the bedroom, his eyes widened, she looked stunning, she walked over to him, he loved the red lipstick that she was wearing; her eyes dark and inviting and her hair dropped loosely down her shoulders and draped down her back. Laura stood in front of him, he was still sitting on the bed with a glass of wine in his hand. His eyes moved down from her face to her firm and beautiful breasts and they lingered there, the sight of her large dark pink nipples sent a warm rush through every vein in his body, they were so pert, reaching out to him, wanting him to touch them, and he licked his lips, his body was insanely screaming out for her, but, he didn't move an inch. Laura took the glass of wine out of his hand and placed it on the bedside cabinet. Then she ran her fingers through his hair, making him smile at her touch, gently she straddled him, wrapping her legs around his waist, then took hold of his hands placing them firmly on her breasts, she wanted him and he knew it, she leant her head back and with her hands-on top of his, encouraged him to caress her breasts. As soon as he started, he didn't need her help anymore, he caressed them then quickly lifted her nightie up, she held her arms up high, so he could take it off completely. Then he kissed her breasts, he had missed them so much, he sucked on her nipples and she moaned with delight. His hand stroked her spine gently up and down, he licked, kissed and sucked her nipples. He loved hearing her sounds of pleasure. His hands went to her bottom and he pulled her closer, she could feel every inch of his need for her, he was so hard, she could feel it throbbing, desperately wanting to enter her. Then she kissed him, at this point they were ravenous for each other.

"I've missed you," she moaned. He continued to kiss her, his lips moving with an urgency from her lips to her breasts as though she would disappear at any minute. Then he looked at her. "And I have missed you too, my darling, so very much" he said. There was no stopping either for either of them, holding her in his strong arms he stood up, her legs still wrapped around his waist, and gently he placed her down on the bed, she smiled, watched him undress, then pulled him down onto the bed, he couldn't keep his hands off her and she shivered at his every touch, quickly she sat on top of him, he cupped her face and pulled her down till their lips met again. Laura couldn't wait anymore. "I need you; I need to feel you inside me right now." Ray eased his erection into her, and she moaned with delight He could feel her tightness around him, so tight that it made him feel like she was holding on to every ounce of him, never wanting to let go. It felt beautiful and precious, if there was a heaven, he was sure, this was what it would feel like. She moved her hips slowly in a circular motion and then threw her head back, he felt her hair, its feathery touch brushing his skin as she swayed around on his erection. His hands went to her hips, and together they moved and fell into a perfect rhythm, he leant up and sucked on her breasts; the scar from her operation was always visible but it didn't matter. They were lost in pure ecstasy and passion and spent the whole night making love, both wanting to fulfil every sexual urge and pleasure they had missed over the last few months. They needed this special time together.

Laura fell asleep in his arms and in the morning, Ray woke first, and she was still in his arms, he loved her so much and would do all he could to look after her, she deserved happiness after all she had been through, he closed his eyes and said a silent prayer: Father, please watch over her and if I'm not there or able to help her, please take care of her. Laura opened her eyes and saw that he was looking at her. "I've been awake a while now. I didn't

Destiny Rose

want to move and disturb you - you looked so peaceful" he said. Laura kissed him, and he welcomed it, his hands slid down to her hips and within seconds they were making love again. Afterwards as they lay next to each other he said, "every morning should be like this." She giggled and went to her wardrobe. They were both smiling, and both felt happier than they had for a while, then her thoughts went to Kay, she would ring her later and tell her how the evening had gone, and she giggled. Ray watched her. "You have a mischievous look in your eyes what are you thinking?" he asked. Holding some clothes in her hand she looked at him.

"Oh, it's nothing important. I was just thinking about Kay and a dance she used to do years ago. I tried to do the dance, but I was no good at it and she laughed at my attempt" she said. He stood up walked over to her. "It sounds like we both have two left feet, because I can't dance to save my life" he said, then kissed her on the tip of her nose and smiled, he added. "But I will jump in the shower first because you take ages" and he rushed to the shower before she could beat him to it, Laura laughed. The next few days were great for them both, he was no longer scared to touch her, and laughter filled the house again. Marcy visited each day and made their meals she wouldn't take no for an answer.

The week later Ray went into work for a few hours. Marcy and Tom had gone out for the day with the church. Kay and Laura were sat at the table in the kitchen talking. The book about Allonywood was still on the table. Laura picked it up and went straight to the page with the picture of Mr. Surringer on. She looked at his image then at Kay and said. "Kay please don't think I'm losing my mind, but I saw this man. Surringer, was in my dreams. I had seen him before, but I didn't know who he was. I was walking Charlie in the woods and suddenly he was standing in front of me, stopping me from walking and then he vanished into thin air" Then Laura went quiet. Kay was shocked and stayed silent. Laura continued. "I just don't get it Kay. I can understand remembering my own memories that I had completely forgotten. I even saw my parents faces crisp and clear, and I had never been curious as to what they looked like before. But I remembered Bret's memories, I saw him in my mind, he was a child. I know it was him. I just don't understand how that could be, or why this is happening to me?" Kay took hold of Laura's hands across the kitchen table and held onto them. "Laura, maybe he told you bits of his past that you have forgotten, and they had resurfaced, you always said that your pasts were one of the reasons that had brought you together. The fact that you'd both had similar experiences as children. You must have remembered his childhood when yours came back to you, and you were reading this book just before you fainted maybe it was still logged in your mind?" Kay suggested.

"I remember an old spiral staircase and a dark corridor at the top of the building." Laura replied and desperately flipped over showing her each page. "Look, there is no picture of a spiral staircase in this book, but I know it was there, I am certain. Maybe if I dig deeper and find out more about this place, I can prove it. I know I am not going mad, why would I be going mad when I am the happiest, I have ever been in my life?" Laura went quiet and held her head low, Kay knelt beside her.

"Laura, I don't think for one moment you are going mad, I believe every word. I just can't fit it all together to give an example of why all this could be happening to you. Never doubt that I believe you, and together we will work it out. I promise. I will take this book and talk to Martin tonight. He will tell me everything he knows about this place" Laura smiled and gave her a hug,

"Thank you, Kay." "You would do the same for me, that's what friends are for" Kay said, and she was right, Laura would do all she could to help her if she was in trouble, or in doubt.

"Forget it now, I will talk to Martin later and we will try to get to the bottom of this."

Destiny Rose

CHAPTER SIXTEEN --- KNOWLEDGE

Kay left it till morning to talk to Martin and when they were sat on the sofa after breakfast, she told him everything Laura had said. Martin heard every word; he was shocked and stayed silent. How on earth did Laura know Surringer's name and about the old iron staircase, she described it exactly like the one in the home, but how would she know? Kay caught Martins look of disbelief and knew something was wrong. Gently she turned his face, so they were looking at each other, and continued.

"I believe her Martin, maybe that breakdown brought on a psychic experience, or some other bizarre, and unbelievable phenomenon. It's the only thing it can be" Martin didn't believe in anything to do with the supernatural. He didn't know what to say in reply.

"I don't know Kay," was all he could muster, she started again, "how many times have we both heard of people having near-death experiences and saying they remembered seeing a bright light or talking to people on the other side. Maybe some things really can transcend the laws of nature and all that is normal or natural? Then she went quiet. Martin was in deep thought, then said. "She isn't making it up and she isn't going mad. That corridor with the door at the end and staircase did exist. Surringer was the master of the home" then he went quiet and held his head low.

"Something happened, something bad, I can feel it" she replied. Martin told her what happened at the home, her heart sank, she was saddened learning what that man had done and

Destiny Rose

how the children were treated and felt sick and her hand went to her stomach.

"It's terrible Martin" she said, he held her close. Kay felt sure now that something unnatural and impossible was going on, and thought, how did Laura know about those things in the home? None of it was in the book she had read it herself to make sure.

"Martin, why is all this happening to her? "she asked. Martin looked at her. "I don't know, but I will stay here with you, until I find out. Let me take over with Laura, I don't want you getting too worried and stressed we have to think about the baby" he replied. She smiled and kissed him gently on his cheek.

"Thank you, Laura would welcome any help you can give her" she said. Then asked if he would keep it between themselves and explained how Ray had only just started to get his confidence back and telling him would only set him back. Martin agreed.

Kay rang Laura mid-morning, Ray had gone into work, she told Laura that Martin would be helping them now and would stay here until all this was resolved. Laura immediately felt a large weight lift from her shoulders. She thanked Kay for helping her through this and told her that although what was happening to her sounded bizarre and something straight out of the twilight zone, she didn't feel scared, for some strange reason she felt strong and as though this was meant to happen.

Kay didn't fully understand what Laura was talking about, but she felt relieved to hear that she didn't feel scared. Kay told Laura that Martin had suggested asking Marcy about her time in the home and see what she remembered? and assured her she would be tactful whilst questioning her. Laura agreed and told Kay to come over at teatime tomorrow evening, she would make them all a meal and invite Marcy and Tom.

The next evening, Laura set the table and made them a roast

Destiny Rose

dinner. She joked that although it was midweek, she really wanted to cook a roast and none of them complained. They enjoyed the meal and afterwards the men sat down in the living room. The ladies sat at the kitchen table with a fresh pot of tea. Kay took the book about Allonywood out of her bag. "Marcy, did you work in this place, Martin thought he heard you mention it?" she asked. Marcy looked at the book.

"Yes, dear a long time ago." "Isn't it a small world because Martin lived in that home when he was a child" Kay said. Marcy's expression turned to sadness. "I hope it was a better place when he was there, than it was back then." Kay shouted for Martin to come and join them. Martin walked into the kitchen, Ray and Tom followed. They all sat down. The ladies were quiet.

"What is it what's wrong" Martin said not liking the deathly silence from the women.

"Nothing is wrong, it's just I told Marcy you were in that home as a child and," - but before Kay could say another word, Marcy said, "It's okay dear, I will explain" and gave a smile. They all sat silently waiting for Marcy to speak again, she opened the book about Allonywood and left it open on the page with the picture of the staff and pointed at the people one by one, "I know them all" she said and called out their names. Everyone was silent and looking at her, then her eyes rested on Tom.

"I worked as a nurse in that place. The children were brought to me if they were sick., but it was a depressing place Tom, it really was. I felt so sorry for the children living there." Tom reached out and held her hand, she continued. "I didn't work there long, and it wasn't my choice to leave. I wanted to stay to watch over the children," she then told them how her office window overlooked the entrance to the building, and about a young girl knocked on the door every Sunday at the same time for over 3 months, her name was Emily, no more than 14 years old, she wanted to visit her brother a lad called Larry who was 7, but Mr. Surringer the head of the house would never let her in, although sometimes one of the staff would take the boy to a window so she could talk to him for a few minutes. That couple of minutes meant so much to them, their faces would light up at the sight of each other. Then Marcy continued, that the staff had been ordered to turn the girl away, refusing to let her see her brother. The week later the same thing happened, but the girl was defiant and she continued to come for over a month and then suddenly stopped coming until one Sunday after being told to leave, she refused to go and she started screaming and kicking the front door. Surringer was furious with her, I stood a few feet away from him, he was vicious with his choice of words. It was horrible seeing the girl crying for her brother, then Marcy went silent.

"Forget about it now Marcy, we should never have brought it up" Laura said, Kay agreed. The men held their heads low feeling saddened at the story, but Marcy was determined to tell them about Emily. With tears in her eyes she said. "I walked away once and forgot about it, but I won't walk away again. I want to tell you all about Emily, I am okay" she said. Ray nodded, as though he was giving them all permission to let the conversation carry on.

Marcy continued, "he was shouting to her he would have her arrested if she didn't leave the grounds, then she went quiet, she must have left. I asked him where her brother was, and why she couldn't see him? But he told me to mind my own business and get on with the job I was paid to do. Then I asked Miss Cordell who did all the books and kept all records how the lad was and why he could not see his sister. She told me Larry had been moved to another home at the other end of the country. I explained to her that every child who left the home, had to have a medical before they left, but the lad had not visited her for his medical assessment. Miss Cordell said they must have got their wires crossed and he must have missed it, but he was gone now. The next day Mr. Surringer asked me to leave the job, I didn't ask why I just walked out and made my way back to the village. Tom interrupted her and said, "Maybe Emily went home to her family Marcy?" Marcy looked him in the eye, "But Tom, why would the boy have been there if they had family, and she was the only one who visited." Then she looked at Laura then to Kay. "I will never know what really happened to her, and I will never forget her face and the sad look in her eyes, she worried sick about her brother. But it's okay I know sometimes we must accept that some questions may never be answered. It's best to put it out of our minds so it doesn't torture us. I don't want any of you worrying about her too, so let's put that damn depressing book in the bin. I will make a fresh pot of tea." She stood up then filled the kettle.

"Surringer must have been there for some years" Martin said, then guessed he could be about 80 years old.

"He could still be alive" Tom put in, Laura's eyes widened, she felt a shiver run up her spine. Something deep inside her wanted to find that man, she needed to meet him face to face, she looked at Tom, "Yes, he could be" she said. Marcy mentioned Mr. Grainger who drove a minibus that would take some of the children away for a weekend every now and again, with Mr. Surringer and Miss Cordell. Kay changed the subject and started talking about baby names.

Back in the motel room, Martin opened his laptop and started searching for people called Surringer. He had no luck searching for the name then he tried Grainger and Cordell, but still found nothing. Then he rang Tony Ratchet, if anyone could find them, it would be him….

Tom stayed with Marcy that evening, and after a light supper, they both sat in armchairs by the fire. Charlie lay down at Marcy's feet, she looked at Tom and said.

"I never should have left, I should have stayed local, Emily she was such a desperate soul" Tom walked over to her and knelt beside her. He took hold of her hand.

"My dearest Marcy, you could have stayed and never found her, that would have made you ill, and if you didn't come back you wouldn't have married your husband or met Ray. We all have times in our lives when we feel we may have done the wrong thing, but maybe it was the right thing. You were meant to Marry your husband, meet Ray and now have me in your life" and he paused.

Marcy looked at him, she had never thought of it that way before, he continued.

"I am thankful we found each other you have brought some light back into my life" Then he went quiet. She gave a smile, big enough to light up the room and replied.

"Ray is like the son I never had, and Laura the daughter I would have wanted, and I am thankful you came into my life, and Charlie. I mustn't forget him." Tom kissed her gently on the lips. Then said.

"I am sure Martin will do all he can to try and trace your Emily, and I feel certain if she is out there, he will find her, now I think we should forget about it for a while. it's been an emotional afternoon" Marcy agreed.

Over the next few days nobody mentioned anything to do with Allonywood again, they didn't want to subject Marcy to anymore unwelcome feelings. Marcy and Tom completely avoided the subject too.

Destiny Rose

CHAPTER SEVENTEEN --- SURRINGER

9am, Sunday morning. Tony rang Martin, he had found Surringer, Grainger and Cordell, and all three were alive but he found nothing on Emily. Martin wasn't shocked by the news, he thought he would have been, but he wasn't, instead he suddenly felt empty. Tony told him that two of them were in separate nursing homes less than 50 miles from where he was based, and the other one was over 200 miles away in sheltered accommodation. Martin took notes.

Tony told him he would be going to see each one, and enquire about Emily and her brother, he would visit Miss Cordell first, and even though it was such a long time ago, she may remember something. Martin thanked him.

"No problem pal, if I can find Emily for your friend and she can have peace of mind, then I'm glad to help."

"I owe you one" Martin replied. Tony laughed and said, Yes, the brunette dancer who always wears red lipstick, she will do as payback." Martin laughed.

Kay woke up at 10 am, and immediately Martin told her the news. She was shocked that they were all still alive, "they must all be over 80 or near that age?" she said. After they dressed, they went down to the restaurant to have breakfast, Kay had toast and coffee, then said, "I can't wait. I am going to ring Laura and let her know, take your time don't rush your breakfast." "Okay and tell Laura not to tell Marcy anything, we don't want her to get her hopes up, it's best to wait and see what Tony comes back with on Emily." Kay agreed, kissed him on the forehead then rushed off. Laura and Ray were asleep when Kay phoned, it was 11am and they were having a lie in. Laura answered the call on the way to the bathroom. Kay told her the news about Tony finding Surringer. She stood still, frozen for a second, she couldn't believe it and rushed into the bathroom. keeping her voice low she said. "I need to see him Kay, please help me?"

"We are helping you Laura, Tony will talk to Surringer after the others" Kay replied but Laura wanted to stand face to face with him, and with desperation in her voice continued.

"Kay, there are questions in my mind and unless I see him myself and talk to him face to face, I don't think I will ever be free of this chaos inside" Kay told her she would talk to Martin and see what he thought about the idea. Laura was quick to reply. "But if Martin comes, Surringer may not talk to us if we are with a man, and this could be the only chance we have of meeting him. We could say we are going for a little break, there would be no harm in it"

Kay didn't like the idea of keeping it from the men, but Laura did have a point. He could be scared off at the sight of Martin, and if a police officer turned in with questions, he might clam up completely. Then she said. "It's okay, don't worry Laura, we won't tell the men about this, we can meet that man together. I will say I'm booking into a spa for a few days. I think the men would welcome the news"

"Thank you, Kay," Laura said, feeling relieved that a huge weight could soon be lifted. "

"You would do the same for me.?" Kay replied.

"Of course, would, without a doubt." Then Kay told her to tell the others that they were treating themselves to a spa break for a few days. They would have to go soon and before Tony visited them.

Destiny Rose

Laura felt nervous and excited simultaneously, Kay felt unsure about meeting him but hoped that after the Laura's psychological problems would disappear. Their phone call ended. Kay did some fast thinking as she made her way up to the motel room.

The next day the Ladies told them about the offer they had received to go on the spa break in out the break in two days' time, and even though the was short notice, the men thought it was a great idea and Marcy felt it would be nice for the lady's to be pampered for a few days.

Wednesday morning came and Ray drove the Ladies to the train station

Lavalipar, was a small village in the middle of nowhere, they would need to change trains a few times to reach it. Kay had planned the journey in advance and as they sat on the train told Laura the information she had found out about the place. It was set in the countryside with the closest neighbours, another village being eight miles away. "He must have retired there?" Kay said. Laura looked at her, "Yes, probably" she replied, and continued,
 "someone like him shouldn't have the luxury of being able to retire in such a beautiful place Kay. He should die in agony, suffering, with no-one to help him." Then she went quiet. Kay was taken by surprise by Laura's comment. Even though the man deserved such a death, Laura was never the kind of person to say something like that, so freely and out loud?

They had been travelling for 7 hours and passed many breathtaking countryside view sand were just half an hour away from Lavalipar. Kay had organised a hire care before the day before,

Destiny Rose

so when they got off the train the car was parked up waiting for them. There was no way they wanted to walk along those narrow country lanes, and although they had a map, they were sure they could end up lost.

At 3pm they arrived in the village and immediately found a picturesque Inn, with a vacant room sign in the window. They parked the car and went inside. Upon entering they found one side was a dining room and the other a bar which looked homely. A small sofa was below the window and three high-back armchairs were set in front of a large open fire.

The landlord was a friendly, middle-aged man he helped them with their bags and told them a bit of local history as he showed them to a room. Kay informed him, they had travelled here to find out about a retirement home for her grandfather.

It was now 6pm and the ladies had rested from the journey. They knew exactly where Surringer lived; he had a self-contained flat in an older person's complex, and Laura suggested they could go and see where the place was before visiting it tomorrow. Kay thought it a good idea.

They drove around the village it really was a pleasant setting, all the buildings were made from natural brick or slate, and nearly all had thatched roofs. The women understood why people would want to retire here; it was a lovely place. The roads were narrow some of which were big enough for only one car, and not a one-way system, but there was plenty of lay- by's for oncoming traffic to pull into, allowing them to pass. They drove over a small brick bridge crossing a narrow stream and went on and soon came across the sign for Reathenview, where Surringer lived.

Laura drove past it slowly and stopped when she was parallel to the tall iron gateway leading into the complex. The gates were closed, and they stayed there for a few seconds. A long gravel drive led down to a three-story high building, which was made from natural brick like most of the houses in the village. The lights were on, but all curtains closed.

Then Kay said. "At least we know where it is now" Laura smiled and replied. "we certainly do!" and hoped tomorrow would give her some answers and put an end to the situation once and for all.

"Thank you, for believing in me and coming all this way. You are a true friend Kay" she said. Kay patted Laura on the hand and replied. "You don't have to thank me, let's just hope, we can put it all behind us soon." Laura wanted to find a safe place to turn the car around, so they could head back to the Inn, and within a few seconds spotted an off-licence on the right-hand side of the road. Kay suggested they pick some bits up to take back. Laura parked the car in a lay-by, just a short walk from the shop. Kay got out, crossed the road and entering the shop bumped into a man in the doorway. "Oh, I am sorry" she said. But he didn't reply or look back and crossed over the road.

Laura watched the man as he slowly walked in her direction, her eyes stayed fixed on him. He was a tall man and wore what looked like a bowler hat, with a long thick camel coloured coat on. His head was held low, she looked at the shop but no sign of Kay then looked back at the man, as he got nearer and stared to ass by the side of her car she put her headlights on, her heart jumped it was him, it was Surringer. He looked at her, their eyes locked, she had no doubt in her mind it was him. Immediately she got out and followed him, as he made his way to the iron gates, she shouted. "Stay where you are old man, I need to talk to you." The man stopped walking and turned around. Laura strode up to him stopping just inches away, and they looked at each other. Then Kay shouted her and rushed to catch up with them. Laura turned to Kay and shouted.

"Stay there don't come any closer" Kay suddenly felt scared.

"Laura, what is it, what's wrong? She said desperately said, and reached out to take hold of her arm, but Laura stared at her wildly, her face looked distorted, she grabbed Kay's wrist and shoved her hand away.

"DON'T TOUCH ME, I AM WARNING YOU, GO AWAY" Laura shouted out. Kay was confused although Laura looked like Laura, the harshness of her voice and the words she used were Bret's. Surringer's face contorted into an evil smile, unlike Kay he saw Bret standing in front of him, not the vulnerable, innocent child, but the angry and damaged adult Bret. Laura looked at Surringer. "YOU, BASTARD, I'M GOING TO TAKE PLEASURE KILLING YOU, YOU FILTHY, PERVERT."

Kay felt sick she couldn't believe what was happening, it was insane. Her mind was in utter turmoil, she looked at Laura, and knew no matter what she was witnessing or might came next she had to stay strong.

Then Surringer shouted, "SO, THE WRIGGLER HAS RETURNED, MISSED ME DID YOU BOY. D0 YOU WANT SOME MORE, IS THAT WHY YOU ARE HERE?" Surringer shouted. Laura stepped closer their noses practically touching.

'When a part of Bret went into Laura, so did his restless spirit, he would have left her alone, however when he left the earth and found out Surringer was not in hell, instead he was alive and well, rage filled him and the only way he could get to him was through Laura, because she had a part of him inside her.. He could use her as a vessel to confront him. He was going to drag the evil old bastard, kicking and screaming into hell where he belonged.

Laura's consciousness had fallen into a deep sleep, she couldn't see, hear, or feel anything and had no knowledge of what was happening around her, somehow Bret had taken over her completely. Then Surringer shouted. "And where is Sir Galahad our dear friend Martin. Will he come and save you again" and started laughing. "I should have found you years ago I left it too long," Bret said. Surringer didn't bat an eyelid and between gritted teeth seethed out, "Years have passed by, yet you never forgot me, my special little boy , I must have meant something to you, like you meant something to me, didn't you?" He didn't have a shred of remorse for what he'd done, he was still evil, but Bret wasn't scared of him anymore.

Surringer's voice sent chills down Kay's spine, her stomach was knotted with nerves and her head was banging through tension. Surely this nightmare would have to end soon. Then she was sick, it was too much for the nervous tension in her stomach, she wasn't sure how much more of this she could take before fainting. Laura spoke again. "You have no idea what's waiting for you down there and I'm not the only one. I am not a child anymore I will always be a young man and you will always be the freak that is standing in front of me. You think you could never feel pain because you are unfeeling, numb, a soulless pit.

You have no empathy for the torture you do to others, and you think you will never feel as they did. But you are so wrong, everything is reversed down there, what you give out in life, you get back in death. The pain you will fee eternal and, it will cripple you forever… Bret's words didn't bother Surringer and he laughed. Then Bret said, "Go on, have a good laugh because this will be the last time you ever get to laugh again. we will make you eat your vocal chords and then your eyes, will never see again, but you will feel you will feel everything that you have coming to you" Then Laura grabbed hold of the collar on Surringer's coat, pulled him closer and looked him in the eyes.

Destiny Rose

"The tide has turned old man, it's your time to feel what true fear is, you are going to burn in hell, and I am taking you right now. Laura's hands reached out to his throat, but suddenly he collapsed onto the floor. Surringer was staring wildly, he couldn't breathe, he clutched at his chest and his legs kicked out, then finally he went completely still.

Laura smiled. Bret knew he had died and took pleasure seeing him suffer, he felt himself healing inside, peace began to fill his mind and soul.

Kay didn't move an inch; she knew the man had died and was scared to speak in case Bret replied instead of Laura. Bret closed his eyes and Kay heard his last words. "Tell Laura I am sorry."

Laura fell to the ground, Kay screamed and rushed to her side.

'Bret had left her body and her mind forever. He'd set her free, and was going to wait for Surringer on the other side'

Kay gently shook Laura. "Wake up Laura please" she cried out, but she didn't respond, she took out her mobile phone, but there was no signal. 'Stay calm, stay calm' she urged herself, then ran to the shop, the shopkeeper rang for an ambulance, then they both rushed over to Laura. "What on earth has happened here?" he shouted as he knelt and checked Surringer's pulse. Kay needed to think of a cover story and quick. "When I left your shop, we sat in the car chatting for a minute, then Laura spotted him through the mirror on the floor. We ran over to him, and then she fell to the floor, I think she fainted?"

There was no life in Surringer, so the shopkeeper turned his attention to Kay. He put his arm around her shoulders. "It's a good job you saw him, or the poor soul would have lay there till morning. Your friend will be okay, seeing a dead body isn't nice at all, and she isn't bleeding from the fall" he said. The ambulance arrived within a few minutes, one of the crew went to Laura, and another to Surringer.

"No pulse here, he is long gone. Looks like a heart attack" the medic shouted. The shopkeeper told them he was from the nursing home and every other night would call to his shop for a small whiskey. The medic checked Laura for any knocks she may had got when she hit the floor, but Laura seemed fine, he took some smelling salts out of his bag and wafted them under her nose, a few seconds passed, and she jumped up in fright. Immediately she saw Kay and felt relieved, "what's going on, why are is an ambulance here, what are they doing? she shouted. Kay put her arms around her and hugged her. "Kay what happened here?" Laura said and remembered seeing Surringer standing on the pavement, but nothing else. Kay realised quickly that she couldn't remember anything.

"Nothing happened Laura, he died of a heart attack. We can speak about it later, let's get of the cold and back to the Inn" Kay replied. A medic checked over Laura, she was fine now. Kay explained their accommodation was only five minutes away, so he gave her the all clear to drive.

Destiny Rose

CHAPTER EIGHTEEN --- THE UNEXPLAINED

They both stayed silent on the journey back to the Inn but when they were in the room, Laura said. "Did you try and help him; did he say anything to you?" Kay walked over to her, she put her arms around her and held her close. "No, he didn't say a word we saw him, we were walking over to him, then as if the sight of us shocked him, he fell to the floor, then you fainted.

"So, I didn't get the chance to talk to him after all, and after all the planning to get here, I am so sorry I dragged you all this way for nothing" Laura replied. Kay cupped her face in her hands,

"Don't be sorry, you have done nothing wrong and whatever brought you here to witness that man's death, might leave you alone and in peace now." Then she kissed her gently on her forehead. Laura smiled, "you are such a good friend Kay, but not only that, you are special, and I'm lucky you are in my life. You are Pregnant, and I have put you through so much. This should be the happiest time of your life and I'm putting all my weight onto your shoulders, I am sorry, please forgive me" They both started to cry and held each other close and after a few minutes they calmed down. Kay took hold of Laura's hand and led her to the sofa, as they sat beside each other, Kay said.

"I am happy to be here, you would do the same for me, but I won't lie and tell you I wasn't scared, because I was, I thought you'd fallen ill again." Laura could see the tiredness in Kays eyes.

"I'm so sorry you must have been worried sick" she replied.

"I was, and we've kept all this from the men, and I couldn't ring them for help. I was so relieved when you woke up" tears began to fall again. Kay was shaking, Laura didn't like seeing her so fragile and hugged her. After a few minutes of silence Laura said. "Kay, for some unknown reason I feel like a heavy weight has been lifted. Maybe you are right, and seeing that man die, has helped me, because before tonight the need to see him was like a constant frantic urgency inside, which I couldn't control, but it's gone, I don't feel it anymore"

Kay smiled, "I am so happy Laura, that tells us both that this trip was worthwhile" Laura agreed.

It was 7pm, Kay wanted desperately to ring Martin, just to hear his voice, but she was too tired and what she had seen earlier was still spinning around in her mind. A good night's sleep was needed, she would ring him first thing in the morning. They were both tired and fell asleep within the hour.

Kay woke up at 6am, she dressed and went downstairs to make herself a drink. The landlord had shown them the kitchen explaining to help themselves while they were staying'

Kay sat down in the lounge and rang Martin; he was surprised to answer the phone to Kay so early in the morning. "Hi what's wrong, is everything okay?" He asked, she could tell from his tone he knew that something was wrong.

"Everything is fine Martin, we're both okay, but I do need to tell you something and please don't be angry with me?" she said. Martin listened, he could not believe she had lied to him and put herself in danger by going to see that man, he stayed silent. "I am so sorry, don't be angry, please forgive me. Laura was desperate, she just wanted to try and get that man's image out of her mind and she thought by seeing him she could do that?"

Martin knew she meant no harm and was only trying to help Laura. Then he said. "I am not angry, I am just shocked, and thankful that you are both okay, but please Kay, never do anything like this again, you must promise me because if something had happened to you both, no-one would have known where you were, you can't do things like this again, and especially now you're pregnant, we both have to think before we do anything that could put you or the baby in danger?" Kay knew he was right. "I swear to you. I won't" she replied. "I'm catching the next train out to you, so stay where you are, I will be there in a few hours," he said. Kay asked him not to say anything to Ray not until they all got back. Martin agreed.

Laura woke at 10am. Kay was sitting by the window. "Good morning, it seems we both slept well last night" Kay said. "Yes, we did, I haven't slept that good for a long time." Laura replied.

Kay lied to Laura, she didn't like it, but she couldn't tell her the truth, because what she saw and the words she heard from Laura and Surringer had been spinning around in her mind all night. Kay told her to stay in bed and nipped downstairs to make a hot drink and some toast, she returned with a breakfast tray, then told her she had talked to Martin, who had promised not to say anything to Ray, and would be here sometime in the afternoon. The news didn't surprise Laura, she'd witnessed fear in Kay's face last night, she had gone a lot further than most friends would have and needed Martins support right now.

Martin arrived at 1pm and a taxi brought him to the Inn. The ladies were pleased to see him. He wrapped his arms tightly around Kay and immediately she felt stronger. "You scared the life out of me this morning!" he said. "I know" Kay replied, and then Laura said

"I don't know what happened last night, one minute I was standing in front of him and the next minute I woke on the floor"

"You are both safe and well and that's the main thing" Martin said. Laura suggested that the couple go up to the room to have a bit of time alone, and she would stay in the lounge by the warm for a while. Martin joked. "You get a real coal fire and I bet we have a radiator up there?" Laura laughed and Kay smiled, it was nice to hear laugh again.

When they were settled in the room, they sat on the sofa,
 "Martin there is so much I need to tell you" Kay said. Immediately he saw the worry in her eyes. "Whatever is it Kay? tell me everything" Tears filled her eyes, but she wasn't going to cry, "I will try Martin, no matter how bizarre or insane it may sound." He took hold of her hand and said,
 "It's okay, take your time and just start at the beginning,"
 "Laura doesn't remember anything about what happened last night, she has forgotten it completely, which for her, truly is a good thing, because something happened last night Martin, that I is beyond all logical reasoning and I will never be able to forget it." she went silent. He felt worried, but he knew she was fine, and Laura was fine so whatever happened it couldn't have been that bad, she took a couple of deep breaths, "Something impossible happened Martin" and she went quiet again. "What is it, my love, what did you see?" he asked, she remained silent.
 "Nothing is impossible Kay but trying to explain something completely bizarre or out of the ordinary, can be extremely hard to explain?" he said calmly, trying to reassure her that whatever it was she could talk to him about it. He put his arm around her, held her close, "let us take the logic out of it. Just tell me what you both were doing and exactly what you saw and together we can try and work it out from there, does that sound okay?" he said, she looked at him, it sounded perfectly reasonable to her, she told him everything about last night, from the moment they left the Inn, up to the moment they fell asleep. She told him what Bret's voice coming out of Laura's body had said to Surringer and what he had said to Bret. She left nothing out, and then she mentioned how he called Bret a wriggler and mentioned Martin

and called him Sir Galahad "It's true Martin, that man saw Laura as Bret and not as Laura. I didn't see Bret but It was his voice coming from her mouth, he was so angry, Bret laughed as he shouted out that you just a small boy had the strength to grabbed Surringer's wrist when he tried to slap you across the face, Bret was proud that you stopped him Martin, you believe me, don't you?" The colour drained from his face, "Yes, of course I do, I just need a few minutes to take it all in, to try and make sense of it all" he replied, and they both sat there in silence.

It all sounded insane to Martin but some things that was said, only he and Bret would know, and Martin grabbing Surringer's wrist only Bret would have remembered that. His heart told him she was telling the truth, his yet his brain was telling him it was impossible to be the true, but he believed her.

"You were right, it is impossible to explain" he said, then he went quiet... She was relieved he believed her and could see he wasn't pretending just to make her feel better. Martin had always believed there was an answer for everything; but his head was wrecked trying to work out how all this could have happened? he stayed silent then Kay asked if he was okay?

"Yes, I'm fine, I'm just feeling as confused and crazy as you must have felt last night, and you were here alone, dealing with it.

"I think my concern for Laura kept me strong and I am glad she doesn't remember any of it, it could have set her right back, and after the breakdown that is the last thing she needed." Martin agreed, "I know love, I hope she can have a little peace now" he said. Then Kay remembered Bret's last words to her.

"He said, tell her I'm sorry, they were the last words he said to me before she fainted? Martin was quick to reply. "We won't be passing his message on, I hope he finds peace wherever he is, but she needs to be left alone now" Kay agreed. She could see confusion in his eyes, she kissed him gently on his cheek, he smiled and said. "I just can't get my head it all, I saw a film once and cellular Memory, and how somebody inherited memories from an organ transplant, but it wasn't a true story and surely that is impossible?" Kay hugged him and said.

"Perhaps we should just let it go, we could go insane trying to work it out, maybe we'll never know what really happened, lets promise each other right now that we both forget everything that happened here and. Laura doesn't remember and we can keep it from Ray and the others, what do you think?

Martin thought about it. He knew they would never know the truth and like so many other things in the world, some things are better off left alone and forgotten.

"Yes, I agree, that sounds like a logical answer to the illogical" They went downstairs and at the bar Martin bought himself a neat double whiskey…

Destiny Rose

CHAPTER NINETEEN --- THE SECRET

It was Friday morning. Martin phoned Ray to tell him he would pick the Ladies up from the train station and drop Laura off at home about 4pm.

Marcy sat in with Ray and when Martins car appeared on the driveway, she dashed outside to meet them. Laura Immedialty hugged Marcy then ran to Ray, threw her arms around his neck, she had missed him terribly. Kay and Martin followed them all into the house.

"How was it, did you have a nice break?" Marcy asked. Kay told her they had a lovely couple of days. Laura agreed. Martin joked, "I wish my batteries were recharged, a few days in good snooker hall, might do it" Kay moaned, " playing snooker or pool; isn't relaxing, how can you relax by playing a sport" she said, Martin laughed.

"It's not a strenuous sport though Kay, it isn't like football or tennis" Kay interrupted. "But it's still using your brain Martin, our brains need rest and won't get any playing snooker or pool." Ray looked at Martin and they both laughed, "Why on earth are we discussing brain resting?" Ray said and continued to laugh. Marcy looked at Ray and said. "Don't mock it until you've tried it, you will be surprised, both of you" Martin muffled a chuckle, he knew she was being serious. Martin and Kay said their goodbyes and headed back to the motel. Marcy went into the kitchen to put the kettle on. Laura went upstairs to put her bag away and Ray followed her. As soon as they were in the bedroom, he gave her a long, lingering kiss. Marcy cooked them a light meal the left to meet up with Tom. That evening Laura and Ray decided to have an early night and so did Martin and Kay who were both completely shattered.

Tony Ratchet was 55 years of age and a police inspector for 20 years. This job he was doing for Martin, he was doing alone. He tracked down Mr. Jonathon Grainger in a nursing home in the east of the country. He was in the last stages of Alzheimer's disease, but he still went to visit him. The old man completely incoherent and no use to him at all. The next person Tony would visit was Miss Catherine Cordell and what she had to tell him would shock him to the core…

Friday evening 8pm, Tony rang Martin. Martin hadn't expected to hear back from him so soon.
"I have some news and it isn't good Martin, are you sitting down? He said. Martin looked at Kay.
"Yes, I am sat down, what is it?" he asked feeling puzzled. Kay saw a worried look on Martins face.
"What's wrong, is Laura okay?" she asked and rushed to his side. Martin took hold of her hand.
"Yes, Laura is fine, its Tony on the phone." She sat down beside him on the sofa and she heard Tony say, "They buried them Martin. They buried the children in the woods at the bottom of the grounds of the old home" Martin held the phone away from his ear for a moment, then put it back, The words Tony said were swirling around in his mind not making much sense and he gently rubbed his forehead. "What do you mean Tony I don't understand?". Kay sat silent. Then Tony told him a forensic team had been working on the land most of the day and discovered human skeletal remains and the whole area was sealed off. Martin looked at Kay, she heard every word and was numb with shock, he put his arm around her, and she started to cry. Tony explained, how Catherine Cordell told him Grainger and

Surringer buried the children and if she ever told anybody they would say she did it and make sure she went to jail. They made her alter records of the children who disappeared. He asked her why she had not told someone sooner. She said she was scared to approach anyone in case they wouldn't believe her part in it. Then Tony went silent, Martin stayed quiet too. After a minute Tony continued. "I am leading this investigation now Martin, they will continue working through the night, I cannot promise you the press won't get hold of this story and as soon as they do it will be on the news all over the country, so warn the people who need to know, before this makes the headlines, and I promise you I will still do all I can to trace Marcy's Emily" The phone call ended. Martin was gutted, he felt deflated, like his heart had been ripped out and somebody had trodden all over it. He looked at Kay, she was broken. He put his arm around her and held her close.

"We will get through this Kay, we will," he said, and he kissed her gently on the cheek. He felt sick at the thought of telling Ray, he didn't want to be the one to break this news to any of them, but he knew he had to. Ray had been through enough already, they all had, and he wasn't sure how much more, they could take. Although Martins heart was breaking and his head felt like it was being pulverised into mush, he would have to remain strong. Martin decided to let everybody rest tonight, because they had all had a touch few days, he would tell Ray but that could wait till the morning. Feeling drained and exhausted Martin led Kay into the bedroom and lay her down, pulling her close, he could hear her sobbing gently, however, he remained silent, there was no need for words.

The next day, Saturday morning. Martins alarm clock woke him at 7am. Kay was still asleep, he didn't wake her, he would leave her sleeping for as long as he could because today was going to be a very long day for them all.

8am and Ray was woken up by the sound of his mobile phone ringing, nobody usually rang him this early on a Saturday? He picked it up and was surprised to hear Martin on the other end, Laura was still asleep, so he made his way downstairs with the phone. Martin told him everything that Tony had said, Ray couldn't believe what he was hearing. He sat down on the sofa and was silent, "are you okay, I am sorry Ray, I wish this wasn't happening" Martin said. Ray heard the sincerity in Martins voice and said.

"Yes, I am okay Martin, it's just knocked the legs from under me,".

"Kay knows, she cried herself to sleep last night. God knows how Laura and Marcy are going to take this, but I promise, I will do all I can to help everyone through this." Martin said. Then he went silent.

"Laura or Marcy cannot know about this Martin; it would destroy them. We can tell them that your contact didn't find anything, and they will forget about it before long." Martin stayed silent, Ray mustn't have heard him properly, and he said,

"Ray, the police sealed the area off last night, they have been all night, it won't be long before the press are involved, so its best they hear it from you or Tom. Kay and I can be there with you if you don't want to do it alone?" Ray closed his eyes, he couldn't believe this was happening, but it was, and somehow, they would have to cope with it. There was nothing he could do to save the women from hearing about this, and he said.

"After all that has happened to us, and each time we have made it through even though the odds were against us, now this! I pray that old woman is just senile and none of this is true, but if it is. Kay being here will be a big support for the ladies. I will

Destiny Rose

talk to Tom and warm him about what might be coming today." Martin said he would ring him as soon as he heard anything else." Then the call ended. Ray was dreading the thought of having to break this news to the women. He made himself a strong coffee and sat at the kitchen table. Then rang Tom's mobile phone.

9am, and Tom was walking Charlie in the woods when he answered his mobile phone. He heard Ray. "Hi Tom, how are you." "Good morning Ray, I'm fine is everything okay, is Laura okay?" It was unusual for Ray to ring so early on a Saturday.

"Yes, don't worry Laura is fine, it's just…." Then he stopped talking, he couldn't find the right words.

"What is it, what's wrong?" Tom asked.

"It's about Allonywood Tom, that children's home where Marcy worked. Martin rang me this morning. Its bad news. The police found human remains last evening, they sealed an area off and are expecting to find more today" then he stopped talking. The news spun its way around Tom's mind.

"This is terrible, are they sure they are human and not animal? Ray told him they were sure. "If any of those bones belong to the children, this will break Marcy's heart, the shock could even kill her, what are we going to do?" Ray explained that Martin would ring him as soon as he heard any more news. Tom made his way back to the cottage with Charlie, his mind laden with worry.

Destiny Rose

CHAPTER TWENTY --- THE END

11.45am and Laura was sat on the sofa. Ray was sat in his chair and his mobile phone rang. He answered it to Martin. He looked at Laura and said. "It's Martin. Tom has suggested we do some fishing with him tomorrow." Laura smiled, she thought it a good idea, then he went into the kitchen, shutting the door behind him, he kept his voice low. Martin told him that Tony had rung half an hour ago and how the police had worked overnight at the old care hoes ground and the news was worse than they could ever imagine, then Martin went quiet. Ray said,
"It's okay. Just tell me?"
"Twenty-six Ray." Martin replied. "What does twenty-six mean?" Ray asked, he didn't understand what Martin was talking about. "Bodies Ray, there are twenty-six bodies." Ray's legs buckled underneath him, and he held onto the kitchen worktop to steady himself, his stomach rolled over and he felt like he was going to be sick. "God knows how I'm going to tell Laura" he said, and before he could say another word Laura was next to him. "I need to tell you something. I don't want to tell you, but I have no other option." "Tell me what? what is it Ray?" Fear ran through her body, he turned to look at her the colour had drained from his face, he looked at her as though he had seen a ghost.

"Tell her Ray, she is stronger than we think, she will help console Marcy when she finds out" Martin said. Ray gave a strained smile and looked at Laura "Okay, I will ring you later Martin." They sat on the sofa, Ray told her everything and she broke down crying, he put his arms around her and kept a tight hold until she became calmer.

Destiny Rose

At 1pm, Ray went to Marcy's cottage. She was surprised to see him at the door, he always phoned before he visited. "Hi, we weren't expecting you to drop in" she said and gave a big smile. Ray was quick to reply, "Hi Marcy, I just wanted a quick chat with Tom about fishing and thought I would surprise you both."

"He is in the kitchen, come on I will make you a nice cup of tea." Tom was sat at the table, he looked at Ray, then said "Marcy dear. I'm going to show Ray the new floats I got. They are in my bag by the back door, we won't be long." She filled the kettle. She said. "That's okay I will bring the tea out to you."

The men sat on a bench in the back garden, Ray wasted no time telling him what the police had discovered, and he left no stone unturned. Tom was shocked, he couldn't believe what he was hearing, then he found it hard to catch his breath and started to cough erratically. Ray put his hand on Toms shoulder.

"Take a few deep breaths," Ray urged. The news hit him hard, it felt like a ten-tonne truck hit him, then he took a few more long and deep breaths and slowly calmed himself down. He closed his eyes, leant his head back and stayed like that for a minute. "We cannot tell Marcy this will destroy her Ray" he said. Ray looked at him. He put his arm around his shoulder,

"Laura knows Tom, I had to tell her just over an hour ago, we don't want to tell Marcy, but we must before she hears it from anyone else, news travels fast around here, Laura will be there for her and you and me" Ray said. Tom asked how Laura had taken the news. "As badly as anyone would Tom, she wants me to take you both back to the house with me, so we can all be together when she hears the news" "Ray replied. "Okay, we can do that Ray, but what are we going to say to Marcy about why we are coming back with you?" Rays mind went into overdrive, then he said. "I could say when I left my house, Laura has messed a recipe up that was going to be our evening meal. Marcy will want to come and help her" "Yes, that will could work Ray" Tom replied...

Ray walked into his house with Tom and Marcy and as soon as Laura saw Marcy, she felt dizzy and held onto Rays armchair.

"Are you okay Laura, you look a little pale?" Marcy asked, as she walked over to her. "Yes, I'm fine Marcy I get like this once a month, its women's troubles," Laura lied because she couldn't think of anything else to say. Marcy walked into the kitchen and put the kettle on, when she returned to the living room, the men were sat side by side on the sofa. There was a deathly silence in the room, you could have heard a pin drop. This wasn't normal something didn't feel right, then Marcy looked at Laura,

"Okay show me the recipe you have messed up Laura and maybe when I save it the house will fill with chatter again" Marcy joked. Laura was puzzled "What recipe Marcy?"

"The recipe for your evening meal tonight, that is why I came over" Laura looked at Ray, and Ray looked desperately at Tom, they had forgotten to tell Laura about the excuse they gave Marcy to get her to come back with them.... Marcy looked at each one of them, then her stare lingered on Ray.

"There is no recipe is there, something is wrong, whatever it is just tell me" she said, then she looked at Tom. Tom looked at Marcy but stayed silent. Laura then said, "I will make us a let's pot of tea" and she went into the kitchen., but Marcy didn't follow her, he stayed put. She could see the worried look on the men's faces clearly now; she hadn't noticed it before. She looked at Ray and then to Tom, "Something is wrong isn't there? If one of you is ill, just tell me" She demanded with desperation in her voice. Tom stood up, took hold of her hand and said, "Nobody is ill Marcy, we are all as fit as you are" he said, then he guided her to the sofa. Ray told them he would help Laura with the

Destiny Rose

drinks and disappeared into the kitchen. Marcy looked at Tom, she couldn't think what on earth it could be. Ray and Laura walked in with the drinks tray, they put it on the coffee table, Ray sat beside Marcy on the sofa, Laura sat in the armchair. She looked at Marcy and said, "tell her Ray" Tom held her hand, Marcy felt sick, 'whatever it was must be bad to have them all acting this way'

Ray began telling her how Martins friend, a police Inspector searched for information about the care home she once worked in, and he had found two ex-members of staff and visited them. Then he went silent. Marcy looked at him, "It's okay Ray, whatever it is, please carry on" He told her they had discovered human remains in the old homes' grounds. Marcy closed her eyes and sat back in her chair. Laura stood up, walked beside her and hugged her, "I am so sorry Marcy" she said and kept her arms around her gently holding her. Marcy patted her hand softly, staying silent for a minute, and keeping her eyes shut said.
"It's the children, isn't it?" she said.
"Yes Marcy, it is" Tom replied. Marcy took in a long and deep breath. They all stayed silent for a few minutes, "I felt there was something was wrong in that place, but I never would have imagined anything like this, how could that have happened right under my nose. I should have never left the area. I should have tried to find Emily, I should have known what was going on., I let those children down" she said and looked at Tom.
"My dear Marcy, you and I have nearly lived a lifetime and although we don't like to think about some things that happen around us. We have both heard news reports over the years and know that sometimes we cannot always see what people are doing, or what they are capable of even if we work with them or live in the same area. They are evil, manipulating and cunning. They hide who they are behind an invisible mask. They can

change their character and appear to be different than who they really are. They could be a Judge in chambers, a street cleaner, politician, and could be anywhere, nowhere is safe from them. Ray agreed. "It is true Marcy, we all would have done the same as you, you must never blame yourself for not noticing something that was being kept so well hidden from you and all the others" Tears fell from Marcy's eyes. Then Laura said, "but there is better than bad in this world Marcy, so many good and honest people and we must never forget that." Life had shown Marcy what Laura said was true. She had met many good people and never a bad one, not until now...

They all stayed silent for the next hour, Ray phoned Martin to let him know that Marcy knew. Martin and Kay made their way over and arrived at 2.30pm. Laura was happy to see them Kay gave Marcy a hug. "It's terrible Marcy" she said. "I know, I know it is dear." Marcy replied.

The ladies sat on the sofa and the men sat in the kitchen. Martin told them; Tony would visit them about 4pm. He wanted to update them, and make sure everyone was okay. Ray wondered if the women were up to it, so Tom, went to ask them.

"I don't think I could take much more Tom" Marcy said.

"Same here" Laura echoed.

Martin heard them and said "If anyone is not up to having the meeting with Tony. It is okay, we don't all need to be here, one or two of us could sit with him" He shouted. Tom looked at the ladies "Sounds good to me." *He* said. Kay looked at Laura and she looked at Marcy, they took hold of each other's hands and held them tight, then Marcy said. "Thank you, Martin and Tom but, it would be selfish for some of us not to be here when others are. We are all feeling the same level of shock and hurt. This is happening to all of us, we cannot run or hide from this. We will get through this by sticking together. What do you say

Destiny Rose

Ladies?" Laura nodded her approval; Kay did the same. Tom gave Marcy a peck on the cheek. "Don't worry, it will be okay Tom." she said.

Tony Ratchet arrived at 4pm. Martin introduced everyone. Ray brought a couple of chairs in from the kitchen, so they could all be seated in the living room. Marcy and Laura made drinks and when they were all settled, Tony asked if anyone wanted to leave the room before he shared the report. Nobody left and no matter how hard it would be, they wanted to know the truth about what happened. He confirmed what Martin had already said, that twenty-six bodies had been found, and the investigating team had worked all day and night and were confident there would be no more remains found in that area. He told them they had checked the backgrounds of the adults involved and they had never worked anywhere other than that place. The team searched the wider area using the latest ground penetrating radar equipment which allows them to take three dimensional of images of bones up to six foot under the ground, and nothing more was found." Then Tony looked at Martin. "The next piece of information I have to tell you is extremely sensitive, will the ladies be okay for me to continue?" he asked. Martin looked at the Ladies and Marcy spoke. "We are ready to hear whatever you have to say Mr. Ratchet, we will be okay, please carry on," and with that, Tony told them a team of pathologists backed up by the forensic anthropologist have dated the bodies. They have been there over a period of thirty years. All but one had died by strangulation, the other was a blunt force trauma to the back of the head" Then he went silent.

Kay, Laura and Marcy were holding each other's hands, tears were falling from them all, they were of in shock." It's okay, we are okay, carry on please," Marcy said. Ray moved over to the side of the sofa and knelt on the floor beside Laura. Martin

Destiny Rose

stood behind the sofa and put his hands gently on Kays shoulders. Tom looked at Marcy. "We are okay Tom," she said. Laura and Kay nodded. Tony continued, each skeleton was male and no older than twelve years of age, and one was and early adolescence female" Marcy looked at Laura, then to Tom, "It's Emily, it has to be" she cried out her and she buried her face in her hands and sobbed uncontrollably. The ladies hugged her. "I am sorry" Tony said. "It's all such a shock" Martin said. Ray held his head down low; he didn't know what he could do to make the heartbreak any easier for them. Tom took hold of Marcy's hand and gently kissed it, "It will take time, but we will all get through this, we will." he said. There was a deep sadness in their eyes. slowly, Marcy calmed down, tony looked at her and said. "Marcy there was nothing you could have done; it would have been like trying to find a needle in a haystack searching for the child. If she had no parents or kin which is plausible, especially with her brother being in the home. She could have been lodging anywhere. Finding her could have taken years. You mustn't blame yourself for what evil people did" and then he went silent...

"It's true Marcy" Kay added. Ray looked at Marcy and said,

"I felt the same as you do right now, when I was working on the force. I often thought if I had done that or this a different way, I could have changed a situation. But it doesn't always work like that. We can't change the past, and we know what happened to them now. They have been found and we can lay them to rest. They deserve to be remembered forever." Marcy looked at Ray.

"You are right" She replied. Ray gave her a hug, "We will always remember them, they will never be lost or forgotten again" she said. "No, never again" Ray replied. Tony carried on giving them information, he was 98% certain the forensic team would not be able to identify any of them because, all records belonging to Allonywood and its residents had burnt in the fire that ripped through the building, no clothes or any other items were found on or near the remains, and there were six shallow graves, some holding more than four bodies. They had remained hidden because, tree stumps and large branches had been placed on top of them, he ended by saying, nobody would ever have known they were there if the old lady had not confessed Everybody was silent, and after a few seconds Tony asked if anybody had any questions. "What happens to Cordell and the other one, and do you suspect others could have been involved?" Kay asked.

"Miss Cordell is helping us with our investigation, she is being rather clear and honest with us, she didn't actually witness anything to do with what happened to the children, and she will be sentenced accordingly. Mr. Grainger on the other hand is in the late stages of Dementia, we can get little sense out of him. Medical evidence will be accepted by a judge and he will be deemed unfit to stand trial. The other name we had, Surringer, died from a heart attack a few days ago. We are not looking for anyone else, then he asked if anybody had any more questions, Marcy asked if a memorial cross, or headstone could be placed around the area to remember the children. Tony said, he would make sure that her wishes were carried out and something suitable be put in place, to remember all of them…

They all felt drained and nobody had any more questions, so the Inspector left.   It was 6.30pm. The men went into the kitchen to make them all a hot drink. They could hear the women talking. Laura said. "The pain we are feeling will stay with us for the rest of our lives. It won't go away. We had to go through this to find those children. They have a voice now; they have been found and will never be forgotten again." Marcy and Kay stayed silent but agreed with her every word. The men returned with

Destiny Rose

the drinks and as Ray put the tea tray down on the coffee table, Marcy said.

"We will have to light Twenty-Six candles in church on Sunday Tom. "Yes, we will Marcy, we will light them every Sunday." Then Laura said. "You must light Twenty-Six plus one, Marcy? Marcy looked puzzled. "Plus, one, why, who is the one for Laura?" she asked. Laura looked at Martin, to Ray, and then at Marcy. "Bret, a friend of Martins Marcy. He is the one, he recently found out that Bret had suffered in that place and never got over it" then she went quiet, "God bless the poor soul, we certainly will add another candle for him."

They all held their heads low...

No matter how much time passed by none of them would ever forget what happened to the children and each Sunday Marcy and Tom lit a candle for each child and one for Bret too.

Laura's headaches and visions completely disappeared, and she never had any Psychological problems again. Her relationship with Ray got stronger, and they wanted to do was enjoy the rest of their lives together. Kay and Martin returned to their lives in Deminick, they married before their baby daughter arrived. Neither of them would ever understand what had happened that evening in Lavalipar and they never spoke of it again.

A few months after the discovery of the bodies. A marble remembrance monument was erected on top of the hill where the old home once stood so that the children who were found, would never be forgotten again.

The End

Destiny Rose

Forever Flowing Free...

Drowning in the savage sea
No-one comes to rescue me.
I am trying hard to stay afloat
No-one in sight, not even a boat.

Fiercely the waves thrash my face
I fight, and I try to find my pace.
Pulling me down into the deep
Fighting so hard for my strength to keep.

The raging waters keep their hold
I am tired, I am hungry, and I am cold
Hold on, hang on, fight on I say
You'll make it through the storm this way.

Beaten, battered, shattered and scared
She hung on and she dared to take the storm for all it's worth
She made it back to land, the earth.

And now she lives just like the sea, forever flowing free...

©2003EBB

Destiny Rose

NOTE FROM THE AUTHOR

Domestic violence and abuse can happen to anyone, yet the problem is often overlooked, excused, or denied. This is especially true when the abuse is psychological, rather than physical. Noticing and acknowledging the signs of an abusive relationship are the first step to ending it. No one should live in fear of the person they love. If you or someone you know is a victim of abuse, reach out. Help is available.

In the US, call the National Domestic Violence Hotline at 1-800-799-7233
(SAFE).
UK: call Women's Aid at 0808 2000 247.
Canada: call the National Domestic Violence Hotline at 1-800-363-9010
Australia: call 1800RESPECT at 1800 737 732.

Samaritans UK: Are there to talk to round the clock, 24 hours a day, 365 days a year. If you need a response immediately, it's best to call us on the phone. This number is FREE to call. You don't have to be suicidal to call us. Whatever you're going through, call us free any time, from any phone on 116 123. Email: jo@samaritans.org
Samaritans USA: In an emergency, call 911. If you are in crisis or suicidal and need someone to talk to call the Samaritans branch in your area or 1 (800) 273-TALK.
Zealand 0800 726 666   admin @samaritanscrisisline.org.au

Destiny Rose

ABOUT THE AUTHOR

The Author is 48yrs. Born and raised in Manchester. England, she has suffered Anxiety and Panic disorders since she was 17, she and wrote her first poem at the age of 18. She discovered writing words was easier than verbally expressing her feelings. She continued writing over the years and began creating stories whilst looking after her 21year-old Autistic Son, raising him as a single parent with help from her mum and dad. Until now, her stories and poems have been gathering dust in a drawer, and she has subsequently found the time and ability to publish them, so is sharing her work which she hopes the reader will enjoy.

Destiny Rose